Mothman...
behind the red eyes
the complete investigative library

Illustration by Natalie "Orbyss" Grewe

Mothman...

behind the red eyes
the complete investigative library

jeff wamsley

mothman press
point pleasant, west virginia

mothman press

©2005 by jeff wamsley
all rights reserved

book design by mark s. phillips

cover concept by sheridan cleland

additional book layout by ashley wamsley

illustrations by gary gibeaut

pre-press assistance by mary skog

photographs by the author
(unless otherwise credited)

press clippings courtesy *The Point Pleasant Register*,
Athens Messenger, and *Huntington Herald-Dispatch*
unless otherwise noted

All rights reserved. no part of this book may be reproduced in any form or means, electronic or mechanical, including photocopying, recording, or by any information storage and retrieval system, without permission in writing from the publisher.

All attempts were made in good faith to properly identify
and provide correct photo and image credits.
Please notify the publisher in writing of any needed corrections.

ISBN-13: 978-0-9764368-0-5
ISBN-10: 0-9764368-0-9

printed in the United States of America

10   9   8   7   6   5   4

mothman press
324 main street
point pleasant, wv 25550

Mothmanlives.com

Dedicated to the memory of my father

Charles Dale Wamsley
1928-1985

Illustration by Gary Gibeaut

table of contents...

Introduction	9
Enter the North Power Plant	17
Archives: Mothman Clippings	29
Where's My Bandit???	47
Archives: The TNT Area Power Plants	55
That Red-Eyed Monster	65
Face to Face with Mothman	71
UFOs Over 30th Street	79
They Were Dressed in Black	83
Archives: UFOs and Men in Black	87
It Was a Bird...a Huge Bird	97
The Chase is On	107
Archives: The Silver Bridge	111
A Case of Campbell's Soup	123
Visions of Mothman?	129
Update: Point Pleasant Today	135
TNT Area—Mothman's Lair	141
Archives: Popular Media	151
Epilogue	157
About the Author	159
Acknowledgments	160

mothman...

Illustration by Gary Gibeaut

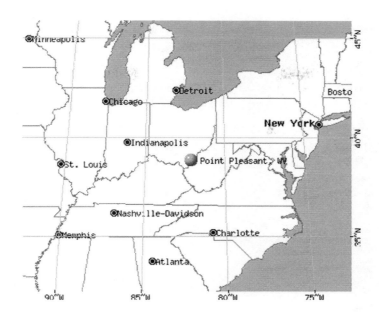

Introduction

What is it about the unexplained that attracts our undivided attention? When no valid answer or explanation can be found to mysteries such as the Mothman, our investigative curiosity kicks into high gear. With hundreds of Mothman sighting reports documented, it is my speculation that there were hundreds of unreported sightings as well. I have sat down with, and listened to, many witnesses that have said that they were unsure who to talk to and wondered what type of humiliation they would encounter from friends and relatives after they went public with their story. Telling everyone about seeing a 7-foot winged creature with large, glowing red eyes during the 1960s in a small Appalachian town was certainly not of the norm...and it would probably shock townspeople even today. I commend the people who felt the need to tell what they saw during this time, but I also have to respect the privacy of those who did not. For those who have remained silent about the Mothman sightings, I only hope that one day they will speak about what they encountered decades ago. As the years flow by, more and more witnesses have come forth to let the world know what they glimpsed in the TNT area or the surrounding area...these are the individuals who I have written about in this new project.

As I mentioned before, there is a small population of witnesses in and around the Point Pleasant area that went virtually unnoticed to the press and the general public during the 1966-67 time frame. It can almost be compared to an iceberg: what you see on the top is only a fraction of what lies beneath the surface. These are the people I am interested in speaking with in detail as to what information they can provide to piece together the Mothman mystery. With each interview or investigation there comes more crucial contacts such as people, dates and names...then the hard work begins.

I sometimes have a problem with the term "expert" when it comes to the Mothman legacy or other unsolved phenomenon. I have never been interested in being billed as a

"Mothman expert" when doing a book signing or attending a Mothman event, for the simple reason that extensive research and interest in a subject does not always guarantee the expert name tag. It is difficult to be an expert of something that has never been logically explained. I may be an expert in my own personal research and compiling witness data, but I have no valid explanation as to what the Mothman or "big bird" really was...and I don't think anyone ever will. I feel that my sole job is to be a direct link to some of the rare archives and eyewitness descriptions, and to pass along this vital information for individuals with investigative minds to digest the content in any which way they choose. As I stated in my previous book, I am not interested in convincing anyone either way: that the Mothman was real or an elaborate hoax.

I will never forget the day about two years ago that an elderly woman in her mid-70s entered the record store I owned and operated in downtown Gallipolis, Ohio. As she closed the door behind her, she slowly approached the front checkout counter where I was doing some paperwork. "Are you the guy who wrote the book about the Mothman?" she softly asked. My first initial thoughts were, Oh no, this lady is going to jump down my throat about all this Mothman stuff she was reading about. (Everyone has an opinion on the Mothman story and I figured sooner or later I would experience some sort of confrontation over what someone agreed or disagreed with.) Surely this sweet old lady wasn't here to start pointing fingers. "Well...I am one of the guys who wrote it (*Mothman: The Facts Behind the Legend*, co-authored with Donnie Sergent Jr.)...can I help you with something?" I said.

"I have your book. I read the section about the Men in Black...they came to my house."

My ears perked up immediately as she then began to tell me how she was visited at her home by a couple of the "Men in Black" when the Mothman sightings were at their peak in 1966-67. Terrified by the knock at her door, she told me she "Hid in the house while watching the strange visitors on her porch." She lived in rural Cheshire, Ohio, a small village about five miles north of Gallipolis and located almost directly across the Ohio river from the TNT area where most of the Mothman sightings occurred. It was the middle of July and these men were wearing black suits with black turtlenecks. She continued, "They were dressed in an odd manner...I watched them leave and walk over a nearby hill...they did not leave in a car."

We stood and talked for maybe 15 minutes or so. For me, any chance to talk to someone like this woman who lived and experienced all that happened here back in 1966-67 is nothing short of thrilling and this story was no exception to the rule. It's a free history lesson, plain and simple. Those were certainly strange times, and to hear the details firsthand always grabs my undivided attention. As our conversation finally came to an end, I thanked her for stopping in and telling me about her experiences. I began to wonder if this was just the beginning of all these firsthand accounts and eerie stories...were there really that many people still interested in talking about what they saw or remember during these now legendary days of the Mothman sightings?

The answers are in the following pages of the stories and words of the people who were integral pieces in the Mothman puzzle.

I am fascinated by fine detail...looking deeper into a story is where I feel right at home. It's not enough for me to hear the basic information because I always find myself picking it apart and finding another story within a story. Questions that go unanswered for decades seem to interest me for some reason or other: the Kennedy assassination is a prime example. I could watch conspiracy-theory TV specials all day long, and I often wonder to myself just exactly what turn would history have taken if JFK would have survived the shots that rang out on that November day. Even more so if Lee Harvey Oswald would have walked through the jail hallway five minutes before Jack Ruby arrived to take his life. *What if...?*

I realize that the Kennedy assassination has little to do with the Mothman legacy, but in a strange way it does when it comes to the question of *what if...?* If concrete evidence and photographs existed of the Mothman (or the huge bird) seen by hundreds, would I be writing this book? The mystery would have been solved many years ago with little or no attention paid to the legend that has now caught the interest of millions. Isn't it ironic how a photograph, or a segment of 8mm film, could have changed history as we know it? Every documentary about historical events like the Kennedy assassination always seem to have one common denominator: the importance of eyewitness accounts and descriptions on what really happened and what they saw with their own eyes.

The Mothman story is no different.

Because the Mothman story and sighting reports are so complex and unusual, it is important for people to realize that many opinions exist as to what people were seeing in the TNT area and general vicinity of Point Pleasant all those years ago. *It is not my intention to favor any one particular theory or opinions of any of the people I sat down and talked with.* As in my previous book, I once again have taken a non-biased approach on any information represented. I feel it is important for all theories to be analyzed in detail. Whether it be the one about some teenagers hoaxing and pulling pranks, or a report of a 7-foot tall creature with wings spanning 12 feet. In every interview I have ever done on the subject of Mothman, the same question always comes up (and I always know it will): "So what do you think it was that they saw?"

To be honest, I have no clue or valid explanation as to what they saw, and I make no reservations about it. I am just an inquisitive guy who wants to talk to all these people who have something to say about what they experienced or witnessed, because I am just as interested in the subject as the next person...to have all the answers would close the book on the whole Mothman subject.

From the beginning, I wanted this book project to offer something for everyone in this regard: whether you believe in the Mothman legend — or *not* — you have to admit that this story is a truly fascinating one. There are many theories to be presented and numerous questions to be asked… to capture the whole spectrum in one project is really an impossible feat because of the unique twists and turns the Mothman story has taken over the past few decades.

The focal point of this investigative work is to dig deeper into the Mothman mystery, through many in-depth interviews and research pertaining to the people who played vital roles in the story itself. In *The Facts Behind the Legend* readers were introduced to the key elements. Sighting reports and press clippings...the TNT area...the Men in Black presence...and the Silver bridge disaster — all of the building blocks needed to piece the Mothman puzzle together. This book will give the reader a deeper and more direct information source that only the witness testimonials can provide.

Since the release of the Sony pictures movie *The Mothman Prophecies* in early 2002, the Mothman story has taken two different directions, and understandably so. One being the actual events that took place in Point Pleasant in 1966-67; the other, the plot and story presented in the movie. I find myself being asked questions about the movie frequently and it becomes difficult to explain to someone from Wyoming — who has never visited Point Pleasant — the differences between the actual events and the movie representation. The movie has undoubtedly taken the Mothman legend to new heights, and it's simply because many have only the movie storyline as their source of information or reference (Hollywood vs. actual events). I often wonder if anyone ever imagined that nearly four decades after the Mothman sightings took place, that a motion picture would literally open the floodgates to millions of people all over the world wondering exactly, "What is the Mothman?"

In *Mothman: The Facts Behind the Legend* many of the basic staples of the Mothman story were represented to the reader in the form of either actual newspaper or press clippings as well as the interview with Linda Scarberry. It's inevitable that there will be some correlation between that book and the one you are reading now. It is not my intention to rehash the same information, but it will happen occasionally. The purpose of this book is to look deeper into the rarest of rare accounts regarding just what these people encountered. I have heard every imaginable Mothman story you can think of...I've heard every theory on who or what the Mothman really was...and that's the pure beauty of it all. Everyone is entitled to an opinion.

What readers do need to realize is that the individuals who sat down with me, and described in great detail what they experienced, are not the type of folks who beat their chests, saying, "Hey! Look at me!" In reality, many of the people I tracked down *avoided the press during the sightings* or simply were overlooked in all the mass confusion.

Since the release of my first book, the opportunities to meet and speak to people who claim to have seen or encountered Mothman have been numerous. But, that is not to say I believe what they are saying is always factual — or simply made up for the sake of grabbing some of the spotlight. In other words, the louder someone boasts, the less I am interested in looking into what they have to say.

The sun sets on day three over the Point Pleasant ramp to the Silver Bridge.

One subject which always arises when people discuss the Mothman story is the horrific Silver Bridge disaster, which claimed 46 lives on December 15, 1967. Many of these questions originate from the people who have seen the movie and naturally are curious about a tragedy of this magnitude. Anyone who lived through this dark period in Point Pleasant's history knows all too well that the memories are still vividly painful even after nearly 40 years have passed. The question many people ask is, "Did the Mothman mystery have a direct connection with the Silver Bridge disaster, and why did the Mothman sightings stop after the collapse of the bridge?"

Recently, I dusted off the old Bell & Howell 8mm-movie projector my dad bought back when I was just about four years old. Every Christmas morning my dad would have me hold a big white poster that he carefully freehanded or stenciled with bold letters proudly announcing "Jeff's (fill in the year and age) Christmas." It seems everyone has those old home movies somewhere in their attic, and I have always enjoyed just sitting and watching those snippets of time captured on my dad's wind-up home movie camera. Besides our family's holiday films, I remember in particular one specific reel containing footage of myself at about age five, alongside my mom and dad up in TNT area looking for cattails that my mom would gather for decorations or home crafts. Watching these films provides a true picture as to what the TNT area actually looked like during the time of the Mothman sightings.

You couldn't pick a more desolate, eerie setting for the reported Mothman sightings than the barren wastelands of the TNT area. Seemingly straight off the page from a science fiction movie set, the TNT area possesses all that sends chills up one's spine, whether walking or driving through the vast landscape of where once stood two giant power plants and rows of concrete "igloos" used to safely store high explosives. The TNT area is just a few miles north of Point Pleasant, but can seem like an entirely different planet if you find yourself stuck in the middle of it.

This is where the many of the Mothman sightings first began, and this is where we begin with this story.

Tank supports made of concrete are all that remain intact today in the TNT area.

Mothman's lair... the North Power Plant, seen here in 1986. The metal smokestacks have been removed from the structure by this time (note photo opposite).

Case Number: WV-35559-101M
WITNESS NAME: BOB BOSWORTH

Sighting Report: TNT Area-North Power Plant
Description: Large winged bird-like Creature
Report Date: November 1966

Enter the North Power Plant

Author's Note: While in junior high and high school, I was a local paperboy delivering the afternoon *Point Pleasant Register* to about 200 customers near my house on 30th Street. In *The Facts Behind the Legend*, I had stated that I used to deliver papers to Linda Scarberry, but it turns out that she was not the only Mothman witness that I had on my

paper route. Being just a kid, busting my butt everyday after school delivering papers, I had no idea back then that some of these people had seen some really weird things up in the TNT area and other places, and to be honest, I really could not have cared less. What I did care about was getting those papers delivered and using the capital that I had earned to buy guitars and the loudest amps possible....

Mothman was not on my priority list. I had grown up all around the legend, and like most people in Point Pleasant, I was fairly used to hearing about the "big bird" and everyone going up to TNT to shoot it. There were two guys by the name of Bob Bosworth and Alan Coates who lived only blocks from each other on my paper route. Bob and Alan were childhood friends and both attended Point Pleasant High School during 1966. Just days after the first Mothman sighting, Bob and Alan spotted something very strange atop the North Power Plant in the TNT area as they drove by on Alan's motorcycle late in the night. What they saw inside of the empty building remains unsolved to this day. If someone would have told me back when I delivered papers to these guys that I would be writing a book with their stories in it years later, I would have probably laughed it off…but I am not laughing now.

Bob and Alan were also some of the witnesses that kept to themselves about what they saw. Bob told me that his father thought he was "crazy" and that "no one would believe him," even if he told them about what he had ran into late that November evening. The following is his firsthand account of standing within just feet of what some have called the Mothman.

Illustration by Gary Gibeaut

So whenever this occurred, this was in November 1966? Do you remember the time frame?

I remember that it was chilly weather because we had on heavier coats. We were still riding the motorcycle but still had on heavier coats, so it was in the fall.

And you and a friend were riding motorcycles in the TNT area? What happened from there?

A friend of mine, Alan Coates, had a motorcycle and he and I decided to ride that evening, just riding around.

And you were aware of some of the Mothman sightings going on?

Oh yeah, yeah. Everybody had heard about it but we always called it the bird. There was a very bright moon out that evening as I recall.

That's what Linda Scarberry also had said on the evening that she spotted the creature.

Oh the moon was extremely bright. We were just riding around and Al said you want to go up through TNT area and I said we might as well.

So you had a license on the motorcycle?

Oh yeah. We rode to Charleston WV one night just riding around.

OK. I didn't know if it was a dirt bike or not.

So we decided to ride up through TNT. We went out what they call Camp Conley road, I think.

There were two of you on the same bike then?

Yeah, yeah. So we're riding out through there and I remember that the moon was so bright that I guess out of boredom Al turned the headlights off on the motorcycle to dodge the potholes by the moonlight. That road used to have lots of potholes before they re-paved it.

And that was the road that is adjacent to the old armory or what are the fairgrounds now?

Yeah. It goes out to the fairgrounds now.

And the North power plant was on your right?

No. It was on the left going out.

OK...OK.

It sits behind where the stage is for the fairgrounds. So we're riding out through there and Al said, "Look at that!" We stopped and up on top on the roof of that old power plant building, it was I believe a three story building, and up on top we seen two big, what looked like red eyes looking at us. We sit there and looked at it and Al said, "You know what that is?"...He said, "Somebody's probably got a couple reflectors nailed to a

Remnants of an old military communications bunker still stand today.

board trying to fool somebody?" and I said, "I bet you're right." So I said, "Let's go up and see what it is," and he said, "Yeah." So we went out there, well we stopped right there underneath the building.

Like the entranceway?

Yeah, we stopped right there and we looked up. Well it looked like these red eyes were looking down at us then. Well that still didn't bother us much because we thought whoever it was just turned the board.

Maybe a couple buddies in there messing around or something.

Yeah...so we decided we were going to grab the front of that motorcycle and turn the headlight on and pick it up and shine it on them. The motorcycle was too heavy. We couldn't get the front end of it up so we decided to go up. Now what you need to understand is that the whole sides of that building except for the last like twenty foot towards the end were these great big industrial windows like you see in the old factories. They were big but they were made up of small panes of glass. Well naturally over the years all the glass had been knocked out by kids throwing rocks and things like that, just nothing there but frames. The moon was so bright that it was shining through these openings and it was making a distinct line toward on the back on the floor there. I'll tell you how bright it was. We didn't have any lights and there were great big holes up there three stories up where equipment and stuff had been removed and we could plainly see those, because I am very leery of high places anyway, but anyway we could see those very plain so we walked back. So we get back and here's like a said this distinct line of moonlight. Well we could make out an outline of something in the dark. The front of my boots were probably a foot from that line and then any further than that and I would have stepped into the dark area.

So you guys were still on the ground floor at this point?

No. We are three stories up and I was thinking to myself how in the world did they get up on the roof of the building because in the process of a lot of demolition work they had removed the ladders that took you up on the roof. I thought that how in the world could anybody get up there? All of a sudden this...I don't really know what to say...whatever I saw...(Alan was right beside of me). It very slowly and precisely walked towards us. Now remember there is glass all over the floor and you can't take a step without hearing a crunch under your feet. We heard it walk and it walked right up and just stayed on the dark side of that distinct line.

Did you notice any red eyes at that point?

No. And I thought about that and I think what it is because there was no light to reflect them. When it turned it seemed to me that the beak or whatever it was wasn't very big. It looked like it was bulky and thick but as far as being long...no.

So it was bigger at the top part of its body than it was at the bottom?

Yes. It came down I guess you could call it pear shaped. That's one thing when I was standing in front of it that impressed me was how much wider it was than me. I would say that its shoulders were at least a foot on each side of me wider.

Almost like someone with shoulder pads on or something similar?

Yeah, but great big but had a very distinct taper to it.

Did you see anything like feathers?

Just a distinct outline, as far as feathers no. I wish I had...I wish I could have got one (laughs).

So you were within 4 to 5 feet of the creature?

The very farthest it could have been was 6 feet.

Did it have any certain mannerisms when it walked? Did it walk smoothly?

It seemed to walk very smooth and very precise. All of its movements were slow and precise, no flighty movements, no waddles or anything like that.

Did it make any type of sound or anything?

No, and its movements were very, very precise and slow. There were no quick movements. It got to the point that if I had taken one step and extended my arm I could have touched it.

At this point did you two still think it was somebody that you knew goofing around trying to scare people?

Yeah, yeah. Here's what we did, because you can't sometimes comprehend what you're seeing. Well it looked very strange so I told Al, "You know," I nudged him with my elbow so he would go along with it, I said, "Al, that's that bird." I said, "I'm gonna shoot it." We didn't have any guns.

You just said it loud enough with the idea that if it was someone trying to hoax you they would come out?

Yeah, but what was supposed to happen, whoever it was, if it were somebody they should have spoke up and said, "Hey man don't shoot, it's me". No. Nothing. It just stood right there. I said it again. I said, "Al, I mean it, I'm gonna shoot it." He said, "Well go ahead." Well I put my hand into my coat like I had a gun. No sound.

So it stayed in the same spot?

It stood right there just as if it were looking right at me.

Could you tell anything about what size this thing was? What proportions and dimensions?

Yeah, yeah. That's something else that I had thought of over the years about. I don't know of any man that I have ever seen that's built that way, well back then, I'm 5'9" and back then I weighed 170 pounds. I remember that its shoulders were awesome. Its shoulders went past me and it had a taper to it like, well I compare it with a robin, you know a bird looks when their wings are folded and how they're bulged at the top and then come down to a taper.

That's also the way Linda Scarberry described it.

Well that's exactly the way it was and it had no long neck like a bird. You know like some of these birds like they tried to say it was. It was just as though it had a head, a large head sitting on its shoulders. The height, I'll put it this way. Like I said I'm 5'9" and I had to tilt my head back a little bit to look to where it's face should be. And it was a rounded head. Well if you can imagine a U upside down, well it was just too big to be a man.

Would you estimate 7 feet tall?

I would say 6'6" to 7 foot, yeah. Because like I say I didn't have to throw my head way back to look up but still you had to look up at it.

And at this point it still hadn't wavered from its position?

No. What was hurting me was my night vision because I was in the moonlight and it was standing just beyond that line right there maybe a foot in the dark but the line was so distinct that the moonlight didn't flood.

Was this in a room or anything or like on a catwalk?

Yeah. There was a big concrete platform things and then out from that the catwalks veered off to the equipment but I remember. Well, in later years I started thinking about trying to analyze what I had seen and I remember that it made no threatening moves whatsoever.

Did it make any audible sounds?

No. No quick or threatening moves whatsoever and had it meant any harm it certainly had its chance right there, towards either one of us. But I remember that any nervousness went away and I started becoming more interested in trying to figure it out. I became at that point very calm. I wasn't afraid. I was unsure and I was a little nervous. OK, so it stands there then it very slowly and precisely turned towards the catwalks. Now these catwalks had been torn up and everything else. They went out to nothing and dropped off three stories down. It's where they had removed equipment so whatever this thing

Illustration by Gary Gibeaut

was turned very slowly and precisely and started walking out the catwalk. Now this catwalk is metal grating. You could see its bulk move and hear its footsteps in the glass right in front of us. And then when it started walking on the catwalk, and I know that sound because I grew up with towboats and so forth and they all have that metal grating on their catwalks. So I'm still to the point that I'm not sure what I am seeing and I didn't want anyone to get hurt. So I yelled out, "Buddy, don't go out on that catwalk. There's no railing it drops off out there three stories down." Never a hesitation. Then we heard that sound like wings. We also heard this sound before we went into the building when we were on the ground but again we discussed it and thought we have on these coats and we could make that sound. But it walked to the back of that catwalk and only at that time for some reason is when we started getting a little nervous. Maybe it started to dawn on us that we were seeing something but we hastily left. On the ride home I remember that I was concerned about the thing maybe following us or swooping down and happening to bump us and at 70 or 75 mph on a motorcycle you don't want to be bumped. One thing that always stuck in my mind all these years is how in the world, if it was a person or someone out to scare us, how they could get up there and then get down that quick and inside while were coming up the steps. It was impossible.

Illustration by Jan Haddox

What was the estimated elapsed time you two were in the building from the time you entered and then the time you exited the building?

I remember it seemed like we stared it for at least 5 or 6 minutes. It was just as though it said, "Well, I'm bored," and left. And all the time I was looking at it and I was that close I wasn't afraid. It was after when I started thinking and that's when I got a little nervous.

So you guys run down the steps. These were the kind of steps that go up and overlap each section?

Yeah, the big concrete step with big railings around them.

Did you hear it as you were leaving the building?

No. As a matter of fact we kept looking back and everything. Of course Al was trying to watch the road but I kept looking. I was 18 or so then, now I'm 57, and I told my wife the other night I would give anything if God or fate, or whoever is in charge, would let me see it again one more time before I die. I would do things differently. I would try to touch it. I just got the feeling when it was in front of me that I was safe and it wasn't going to hurt me. And I have over the years. You know you just wonder about things. I have talked to other people and the only people that were ever hurt by it were people that would run and fall over top of something.

So at this point in time you guys had gotten on the motorcycle and took off and were heading back towards Point Pleasant? Did you think of going to the police or anything?

No. What were they going to do? (Laughs). Well as I remember there was a state cop who seen it one evening and it scared him as bad as everyone else. Back then it was a different period of time. Half of the town thought I was crazy.

So Alan was pretty scared by the whole deal too then?

Alan was a pretty calm guy. I think he felt like I did, kind of uneasy and we should be getting out of there.

And you guys talked about it between yourselves?

Oh yeah, but you know, we were a couple of kids.

Did you tell any of your family or friends about this?

Oh yeah. Of course my dad told me I was seeing things.

Did you know any of the other witnesses at that time like Linda Scarberry, Marcella Bennett or Tom Ury?

Oh yeah. I knew Roger Scarberry and Steve Mallette. Back in those days if you were a kid and had $5 or $10 it was a good amount of money. We were up at Tiny's drive-in one evening after they had seen it. I told Roger Scarberry I would give him $5 to take me up there and show me where they had seen that thing at. I remember Linda Scarberry and she always seemed like a good stand up lady. I think she's the type of person that whatever she tells you is exactly the way it was. She was a good decent sort.

Had you and Alan had already seen it when you asked him this?

No. And he said he wouldn't do it.

And the fact that there were over 100 reported sightings and probably another 100 that were never reported.

Well over by where Walmart and the trailer park and all that is now, there used to be an airport there, a little grass airport.

Strange plane turns out to be 'bird'

POINT PLEASANT — Is it a plane? No, it's a bird.

This was the conclusion reached by five area pilots, who spotted Point Pleasant's "bird" yesterday afternoon in broad daylight and for an instant mistook it to be a plane.

Everett Wedge of Point Pleasant, Henry Upton of Leon, and Leo Edwards, Ernie Thompson and Eddie Adkins, all of Gallipolis, Ohio, were gathered yesterday at 3 p.m., when one man in the group commented on the way a plane was making a landing.

He called out, "See that crazy man coming in, in a downwind in that plane."

The others glanced up at about the same time, and then all of a sudden, they all realized it wasn't a plane, but a bird.

While all members of the group are avid hunters, they agreed they had never seen anything that looked quite like the "bird" they saw yesterday.

Wedge said they sighted it about 300 feet off the ground along the Ohio River bank and they watched it until it was out of sight. All estimated the flying creature to be traveling 70 miles an hour.

The most outstanding characteristic they noticed was the unusually long neck, which was estimated to be about 4 feet in length.

The men substantiated evidence that it was a sandhill crane, as identified earlier by Robert L. Smith, a West Virginia University professor.

Once it was out of sight, Wedge hurried to get his camera, boarded his plane and flew along the river toward Huntington in an attempt to flush it out, but apparently was unsuccessful.

Now Everett Wedge was at this airport when they thought that it was a plane coming in?

Yeah, that's the story, and they claim some of the boys were practicing some of their landings during the evening and they seen what they thought was a plane coming in and one of them said, "Well, what's this nut doing?" I guess they were pilots and knew he shouldn't be coming in the way he was. Well then, all of a sudden, the wings started flapping and they knew right away it wasn't a proper aircraft. To this day the only thing I can say if someone asks me did you see the bird? I've got to say bottom line is I either seen it or I saw the biggest, bravest man I've ever seen in my life. One of the two.

Can you tell me anything about the hotbed of UFO sightings here in Point Pleasant at this time?

You couldn't believe the amount of people that came to town. Well to start with there was some guy who came to town who was supposed to be some kind of scientist or something. This guy was supposed to know all about animals and birds and all that (note: the person he is speaking about was a professor from West Virginia University) and as far as I'm concerned he insulted all of us because he said, "Well, it's nothing but a Sandhill crane". Well the deal is it resembled a Sandhill crane in NO way whatsoever. A Sandhill crane is a tall, long legged bird with a long neck and a beak. You can see a whole herd of them out here at the Columbus Zoo. Had it been a Sandhill crane at that age I tell you what we would have done. We would have grabbed it by the beak and grabbed it by the neck. Al would have grabbed its legs and we would have carried it out of there. But in no way was it a Sandhill crane. That was an insult. That to many other people and me. To think that we were that *stupid* was an insult to us. I am sure the man didn't mean any harm...he was probably asked for his help and he voiced his opinion. But still to think that we would not know the difference between something that we had seen and a Sandhill crane.

That is a theory, and with the Mothman legacy there are so many theories and different perspectives, and that's what's interesting about it.

One of the stories from back then was about this great big reservoir that sits on a hill out in TNT. Now this reservoir is so big you could float a towboat in it if it were filled with water. Out of this reservoir are tunnels that run everywhere. There was the South Power Plant and then the power plant where we had seen what we seen. Supposedly people reported an object hovering over those three points. It would hover over the reservoir for awhile then it would move to one power plant and then to the other power plant, almost in a pyramid deal. Well the Mothman had been seen in at all three of those places. One fellow felt that it was sent here for observation for some reason or possibly escaped and they were back to pick it up. Now that's another theory. I think the one that upset many people is they tried to say the Mothman made the bridge fall. Anybody who knows about metal and metal fatigue needs to remember that when that bridge was built they weren't mind readers. They didn't know the weight over the years of these trucks and things. It's just that the pins sheared and the straps broke and there it went.

But didn't many of the Mothman sightings decrease after the collapse of the Silver Bridge?

Yes.

Believe A Sandhill Crane?

By RALPH TURNER

The case of the Mason County monster may have been solved Friday by a West Virginia University professor.

Dr. Robert L. Smith, associate professor of wildlife biology in WVU's division of forestry, told Mason Sheriff George Johnson at Point Pleasant he believes the "thing" which has been frightening people in the Point Pleasant area since Tuesday is a large bird which stopped off while migrating south.

"From all the descriptions I have read about this 'thing' it perfectly matches the sandhill crane," said the professor. "I definitely believe that's what these people are seeing."

Since Tuesday more than 10 people have spotted what they described as a "birdman" or "mothman" in the area of the McClintick Wildlife Station.

They described it as a huge gray-winged creature with large red eyes.

Dr. Smith said the sandhill crane stands an average of five feet and has gray plumage. A feature of its appearance is a bright red flesh area around each eye. It has an average wing spread of about seven feet.

"Somebody who has never seen anything like it before could easily get the impression it is a flying man," he said. "Car lights would cause the bare skin to reflect as big red circles around the eyes."

While such birds are rare to this area, Dr. Smith said this is migration time and it would not be too difficult for one or more of the birds to stop off at the wildlife refuge. There are no official sightings of such birds in West Virginia, although there have been unconfirmed reports in the past, he added.

The birds are rarely seen east of the Mississippi now except in Florida. Distribution mainly is in Canada and the population is increasing in the Midwest. They winter in Southern California, in Mexico and along the Gulf Coast.

According to one book, the sandhill crane is a "fit successor" to the great whooping crane which is almost extinct. The book states that the height of the male when it stands erect is nearly that of a man of average stature, while the bird's great wings carry its compact and muscular body with perfect ease at a high speed.

Dr. Smith said that while the birds are powerful fliers they cannot match the 100 mph speed one couple reported the "thing" attained when pursuing their car.

Dr. Smith warned that while the sandhill crane is harmless if left alone, that if cornered it may become a formidable antagonist. Its dagger-like bill is a dangerous weapon which the crane does not hesitate to use when at bay and fighting for its life. Many a hunter's dog has been badly injured, he said.

Some of those who reported seeing the "monster" remembered best the eerie sound it made. The description of the sandhill crane also fits there.

"The cry of the sandhill crane is a veritable voice of nature, untamed and unterrified," says one book on birds. "Its uncanny quality is like that of the loon, but is more pronounced because of the much greater volume of the crane's voice. Its resonance is remarkable and its carrying power is increased by a distinct tremolo effect. Often for several minutes after the birds have vanished the unearthly sound drifts back to the listener, like a taunting trumpet from the underworld."

Meanwhile, for the fourth night in a row, an area of the wildlife station again was clogged Friday night with the curious searching for the "thing."

The latest reported sighting came Friday morning from two Point Pleasant volunteer firemen, Captain Paul Yoder and Benjamin Enochs.

"As we were going into the picnic area in the TNT area, Paul and I saw this white shadow go across the car," Mr. Enochs reported.

"This was about 1:30 a.m. Paul stopped the car and I went into the field, but couldn't see anything. I'd say this definitely was a large bird of some kind."

Meanwhile, authorities issued a warning to "monster hunters."

If the "thing" is a migratory crane they had better not shoot it. Migratory birds of all kinds are protected by federal and state wildlife laws.

Sheriff Johnson said he would arrest anybody caught with a loaded gun in the area after dark.

There were earlier reports of armed people in the area.

Sheriff Johnson also warned that the scores of persons searching the abandoned powerhouse in the TNT area after dark risk possible serious injury.

You mentioned to me about your girlfriend's dog and its odd behavior one evening during the Mothman sightings.

Yes. My girlfriend at the time was Diane Grimm whom I later married. She lived at her parent's house on Mount Vernon Avenue. I would walk down to her house and we would stay up late watching movies till midnight and one o'clock sometimes. When I would leave to walk home to my parent's house on Chandler Drive she would let her dog Shep (a collie) loose and he would stick right with me. When we would get to my parent's house he knew that I would go in and get him a big piece of bologna. He would lay on our porch and wait for me to hand him that bologna. He would eat it, rest a few minutes and then head back home. He wouldn't miss that for anything. He liked that bologna.

Was this close to the time that you and Al had been in the North power plant?

Oh yeah. As a matter of fact it was a matter of days after. That's why I still was feeling a little uneasy. So she turns Shep loose and he and I start up the road and we get about a block and a half away. Now Mount Vernon is very well lit. It's double lane and has the grassy island in the middle. So we're walking and all of a sudden he stops. I mean he stops dead and he starts whimpering. I looked down and said, "What kind of spell are you having?" He just would not move. I said, "Come on, Shep." He wouldn't do it. He kept looking around and whimpering and he turned around and I mean he moved. He went back to the house as quick as he could. Well I didn't see anything so I continued to walk home. The next day I found out that a family on Mount Vernon who were up late had seen the Mothman on that island walking around. They then called their neighbors. I think there were three different families who seen it.

So the dog went back to your girlfriend's house?

Yes...it went back to Diane's house as quick as it could go.

And you walked on home then?

Yeah. I didn't see anything.

ARCHIVES:
Mothman Clippings

Four Pt. Pleasant Car Occupants See 'Bird-Like Creature'

PT. PLEASANT, W. Va. (UPI)—Two Pt. Pleasant couples told police Wednesday their car was followed about midnight by a "bird-like creature" 6-7 feet tall with red eyes and a 10-foot wingspan.

Steve Mallette and Roger Scarberry told Mason County Sheriff's deputies they were riding with their wives near the McClintic Wildlife Reserve when they first encountered the "thing."

Mallette said it was large, measuring as much as six or seven feet, was grey in color and its eyes were two inches in diameter. He said the eyes "glowed red" when the car headlights were put on them near an abandoned power plant.

Then, Mallette said the "thing" took off, making a flapping noise, and traveled at high speeds, "at about 100 miles an hour." Mallette added "it was a clumsy runner."

"I'm a hard guy to scare," Scarberry told newsmen, "but last night I was for getting out of there."

"If I'd seen it myself, I wouldn't have said anything about it, but there were four of us who saw it," Scarberry said.

After the first sighting, the men said, the "thing" glided along above the car until their car reached W. Va. Route 62. Then it disappeared.

The four drove to downtown Pt. Pleasant. "When we turned around there it was again. It seemed to be waiting on us," Mallette said. They went to the city limits and saw the creature again. When the car headlights were put on it, it scurried into a field and disappeared.

"It's apparently afraid of light," Mallette said.

Sheriff Deputy Millard Holstead, investigating the report, said he was not discounting the story. He emphasized that none of the four had been drinking.

Even Holstead said he saw a "cloud of dust" near the old power station "and it could have been the bird."

Residents were upset and the speculation was that "the thing" lives in one of the abandoned boilers of the power plant. "There are pigeons in the buildings, but not in one," Mallette said, theorizing the thing they saw might live in it.

REQUEST MEETING
SEOUL (UPI)—The 233rd meeting of the Military Armistice Commission will be held today at Panmunjom, the United Nations command said this week. The meeting was requested by the North Korean Communists.

SUPPLYING SUBMARINES
NEW DELHI (UPI)—The Indian Parliament was told this week that Communist China has agreed to supply Pakistan with three submarines.

Defense Minister Swaran Singh said also that Pakistan had placed orders for submarines with France.

Also in 1806, the first magazine published by college undergraduates appeared in New Haven, Conn., the Yale "Literary Cabinet."

Mason County has 'Flying' Mystery

11-18-1966

PT. PLEASANT, W. Va. (UPI)—The mystery of the flying "whatever it was" continued here Thursday.

Four more people reported seeing a huge, bird-like creature with red eyes. And in Doddridge County, more than 100 miles to the north, a farmer feels his German Shepherd was "dognaped" by the beast.

Mason County Sheriff George Johnson said he does not discount the stories of Steve Mallette and Roger Scarberry and their wives. All four swear they saw the creature three times late Tuesday and early Wednesday near an abandoned power plant five miles north of here.

Raymond Wamsley and his wife, Marcella Bennett and Ricky Thomas told Johnson they saw it too, in the same general area.

Johnson says he feels whatever everyone saw was nothing more than a "freak Shitepoke," a large bird of the Heron family. The Shitepoke or Shag as it is sometimes known, is the smallest Heron in the Western Hemisphere.

No one, however, could explain how a Shag or similar large bird could fly 100 mph as Scarberry and Mallette said the one they saw did. All four said they would take lie detector tests.

At a farm in Doddridge County near the Harrison County community of Salem, contractor Newell Partridge said he saw something with eyes like "red reflectors" in a meadow near his home. He sighted this "thing" about 90 minutes before the Pt. Pleasant incident.

Partridge said his television set began acting up, "sounding like a generator," and his $350 German Shepherd, Bandit, started "carrying on something terrible."

After the dog had howled for some time Partridge said he opened the door and shined a flashlight into the field where the "reflectors" were seen.

The dog's hair stood straight up, Partridge said, and the animal then went after the reflectors. The dog never returned and no trace of it was found.

Partridge and his wife said the dog had never stayed away from home for more than 15 minutes in the last three years.

'Flying Man' Seen Here, Man Claims

A Kanawha Countian said Thursday that he saw a "flying man" similar to that reported Wednesday by residents of Mason County.

Kenneth Duncan of Blue Creek said he saw something that "looked like a brown human being" Saturday in a wooded area at Reamer near Clendenin.

"It was gliding through the trees and was in sight for about a minute," Duncan recalled.

At the time, he said, he and four other men were digging the grave of his father-in-law, Homer Smith of Blue Creek, who was buried Sunday.

The object disappeared before others in the group saw it, Duncan said. Others were Robert (Bob) Lovejoy of Allen, Mich., formerly of Campbells Creek, William (Bill) Poole of Allen, Mich., Andrew Godby of Blue Creek and Emil Gibson of Quincy.

Mason County residents reported seeing the "flying man" at night. They described him as being 6 feet tall with a 10-foot wingspan.

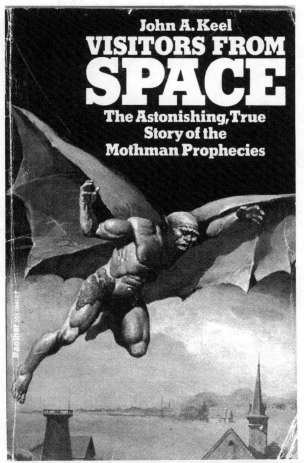

mothman...

Roane County High School teacher George Dudding points to a drawing of the TNT area where Mothman was first sighted in 1966. Dudding was a sophomore at Point Pleasant High School at the time.

Courtesy of The Roane County Recorder, *this clipping documents the experience of George Dudding, who attended PPHS in 1966 with the original Mothman witnesses.*

Memories of Mothman

Dudding was in Pt. Pleasant when sighting took place

By Jim Cooper
EDITOR

The current feature film "The Mothman Prophecies" has generated excitement over the mythical Mason County monster that hasn't been experienced since... well, since George Dudding was a student at Point Pleasant High School.

"There was a lot of excitement," said Dudding, a 16-year-old sophomore when several people claimed to have seen Mothman in the fall of 1966. "We believed they had seen something up there."

Up there was a mysterious tract of land outside of Point Pleasant known as the TNT area. Two couples were in the isolated area late one night when they were supposedly confronted by a seven to eight foot tall creature they described as half human and half bird with glowing red eyes.

Dudding recalls that the terrified couples ran to their car and made it to what the locals called Ohio River Road. The creature reportedly took off vertically and pursued the vehicle all the way to the city limits during a chase that was said to have reached 100 miles an hour.

The couples reported what had happened to a deputy sheriff, who returned with them to the scene but could find no trace of what later was dubbed Mothman. An eerie high-pitched whine came over the police radio, though, Dudding said, a typical feature of subsequent sightings.

Now a teacher at Roane County High School, Dudding can recall the events that followed Mothman's first appearance.

"I believe it was the next night that things fired up again," he said.

Dudding said a family went to visit friends who lived in the TNT area, an approximately 1,000-acre site where the government manufactured explosives during World War II. They got out of their car and Mothman stepped in front of them. They rushed to the house and locked the door.

"They said it came on the porch and even tried to look in the windows," Dudding said. "They say the woman is bothered by the whole thing yet today. It was supernatural, something they couldn't explain."

More sightings were reported and media descended on the area.

See MOTHMAN, back page

Mothman

From page 1A

An article written at the time was featured in a recent special about the phenomenon televised on the FX network. Dudding watched the show and was surprised to notice a familiar name.

"It was 'Search for the Mothman,'" Dudding said. "I could read part of the newspaper account and it mentioned Roger Scarberry and Steve Mallette. I said 'Hey, I have a textbook that once belonged to that guy.'"

Mallette, one of the first people to report seeing Mothman, was ahead of Dudding in high school. One of his old history textbooks eventually was passed down to Dudding, who kept it after purchasing it from a friend for 50 cents.

"It was in bad shape and it was discontinued so I couldn't sell it," he said. "It was the only textbook I kept. It was at my Dad's house when he died in 1980 and since then it's been on a shelf in my basement."

Dudding said he had intended to give the book to Eugene Rayburn, the friend he had purchased it from, but never got around to it. It had been all but forgotten on the shelf until the television show.

As he leafed through the old textbook, Dudding came to page three. What was there, just below the Chapter 1 heading "The Study of Modern Problems," was a crude drawing of Mothman — probably drawn by an actual eyewitness.

"When I got to that page I couldn't believe it," Dudding said. "Back then, I didn't pay any attention to it."

But now the renewed interest in Mothman has stirred Dudding to recall growing up near Point Pleasant on a farm just a couple of miles from the TNT area. He recently saw the movie starring Richard Gere because it is based on events that happened where he grew up.

"I was disappointed they didn't film it in my hometown," Dudding said of the movie shot in Pennsylvania, adding that he enjoyed watching it nonetheless. The movie's link between Mothman and the December 1967 fall of the Silver Bridge in which 46 people died was a stretch, he said, although someone had reported seeing the creature flying around the bridge some time before the collapse.

Dudding thinks Point Pleasant will receive a short-term boost in tourism as a result of the Mothman's resurgence and says he plans on purchasing a Mothman T-shirt.

But he already has a unique souvenir in the eyewitness drawing of Mothman — a creature explained by some as a large crane and by others as something from outer space, a product of toxic waste in the TNT area, the curse of the Shawnee chieftain Cornstalk or a prophet of doom.

"Well, it's hard to say. I'm not really sure what it was," Dudding said. "It's a mystery to me."

George Dudding's old history textbook from Point Pleasant High School includes an eyewitness' drawing of Mothman.

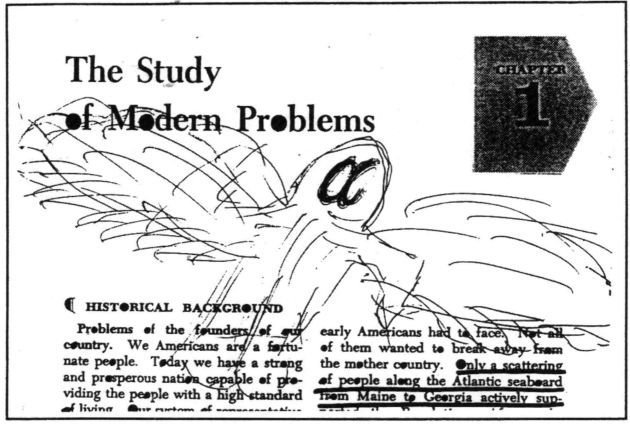

George Dudding's old history textbook from Point Pleasant High School includes an eyewitness' drawing of Mothman.

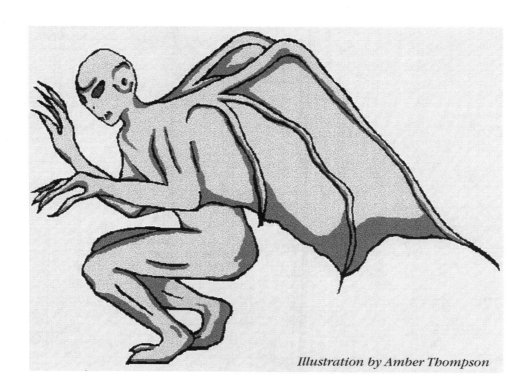

Illustration by Amber Thompson

Mothman and UFOs remain unexplained

The 30-year-old legend of the Mason County Mothman isn't what I remember most about those strange times.

Reporter Bob Withers wrote in Sunday's Herald-Dispatch about the sightings of the strange bird-like creature in and around the abandoned West Virginia Ordnance works just north of Point Pleasant.

I was a young upstart at this newspaper at the time, and I remember the stories about the big bird.

But what I remember most were the other sightings — scores of them that lasted through the late fall and early winter of 1966 and into 1967.

Dave **PEYTON**

The number of Mothman sightings couldn't hold a candle to the number of other unidentified flying objects sighted in the skies of eastern Cabell, Mason and parts of Putnam counties during that same period of time.

Call it mass hysteria if you want, but I happen to believe there was something to the stories reported by the many people who called The Herald-Dispatch with tales of brilliant lights in the sky and saucers hovering over their rural homes, then zipping away into the night sky at the speed of light.

The "saucer sightings" began about the same time the big critter was sighted at the ordnance plant.

But the UFO sightings occurred east of Milton in Cabell County, along the Kanawha River in Putnam and Mason counties and along the Ohio River from about Greenbottom upriver to Point Pleasant.

At first, our crusty old city editor, Eddie Oliver, ignored the calls from scared and frantic people who reported seeing brilliant lights above their homes and what appeared to be hovering spacecraft.

But eventually, there were so many calls, they could no longer be ignored. Eventually the calls became so numerous we had to set up a special "UFO desk" to take all of them.

The story of Mothman was big, but the continuing stories of UFO sightings took up even more newspaper space.

The folks calling these reports into our newsroom were not kooks. Many began their conversations with the words, "I've never called a newspaper in my life about anything, but I have to tell you what I just saw over my house."

A few were in tears, obviously frightened by what they had seen. I heard more than once "Believe me, I'm a Christian, and I'm not crazy."

A close friend who lived in the area near Apple Grove was driving home in the pre-dawn hours one morning and said he saw a saucer hovering over a power line stretching across the Ohio River. It appeared to be connected to the big power line by a lighted rod, as if it were fueling itself on electricity from the line, he said.

Then there was the man in Catlettsburg (I forget his name) who invented what he said was a flying saucer detector: a device he created using a magnet, wires, a battery and a buzzer. When flying saucers were in the vicinity, he said, it disturbed the magnetic waves, which set off the buzzer, he contended.

I'm not sure his device ever worked, and I'm not sure how serious he was. But for me, this period was when I first began believing that UFOs were real.

Then, as quickly as they appeared, they were gone. One night, there were a dozen sightings. The next night, none.

The UFOs disappeared, as did the Mothman. But for lots of folks, both changed the way we look at the strange and the unexplained.

Dave Peyton is a columnist for The Herald-Dispatch. His telephone number is 526-2790 and his address on the Internet is dpeyton@access.eve.net.

Professor Says Moth-Man Could Be Large Crane

A big bird with a nasty disposition when aroused. That's the Grus Mexicana, or more commonly called, the sandhill crane.

A West Virginia University scientist suggests that the "moth-man" spotted by several people near Point Pleasant was this rare bird.

Robert Smith, associate professor of wildlife biology at WVU, told Mason County Sheriff George Johnson that the descriptions of eye-witnesses fit the huge sandhill crane, second largest of the crane family in America. Only the even rarer whooping crane is larger.

Mr. Smith noted that the sandhill crane is about as tall as a man when standing, and in flight its wings spread out to about seven feet. It has a large bill, and it will use it to attack small animals or even human beings if molested.

The sandhill crane's breeding ground generally is considered the northern part of the U. S. and southern Canada, but it is seldom seen east of the Mississippi river. The bird is migratory and winters in southern California, Mexico or along the Gulf Coast.

Mr. Smith said the behavior described by witnesses, such as following their automobiles, has been observed in the sandhill crane.

Reference books say the large bird has been known to attack hunting dogs and wound or kill them with its long, sharp beak. Attacks on human beings also have been recorded.

Smith was of the opinion there has been no previous sightings of the large bird this far east. He said it may have followed migrating geese or other waterfowl to the McClintic Wildlife Station, a favored stopping place for migratory fowl.

Persons sighting the strange bird perhaps better think twice before trying to shoot or harm it. Migratory birds of all kinds are protected by federal wildlife laws.

Reporter's night went by without Mothman sighting

By BOB WITHERS 1/13/02
The Herald-Dispatch
bwithers@herald-dispatch.com

HUNTINGTON — Ralph Turner, a professor of journalism and mass communications at Marshall University, was a reporter at The Herald-Dispatch when the Mothman story broke in November 1966.

Turner

A few days after the first sighting, Turner came up with a bright idea — a reporter should spend the night in the solitary area near Point Pleasant, W.Va., where Mothman was first reported, and write about what he or she sees.

"It was a hot thing at the time, a salient issue," Turner says.

"I don't know if many people took it seriously, but it was a good conversation piece. We wanted to bring it to some kind of conclusion."

Herald-Dispatch City Editor Bill Wild went for the plan, and assigned the story to Turner and reporter/photographer Mike Hoback.

"I remember talking to people in the wee hours of the morning," Turner says. "I also remember being cold and damp and feeling slightly foolish."

File photo/The Herald-Dispatch
This illustration of a sandhill crane accompanied one of Ralph Turner's November 1966 stories in The Herald-Dispatch about Mothman.

But Turner and Hoback kept their warm coats on and talked to reputed eyewitnesses in nearby homes. Then they spent the rest of the night wandering around in the remote area once occupied by the sprawling West Virginia Ordnance Works.

"What I remember most was

> "I never really believed there was such a thing as Mothman."
>
> **Ralph Turner**
> Marshall journalism professor and former Herald-Dispatch reporter

the chill, the fog, the mist in the air, and the vastness of that TNT area," Turner says. "It would have been a good place to make a Dracula movie."

Turner believed there had to be some kind of reasonable explanation for the sightings, but admits he did not find it.

"I never really believed there was such a thing as Mothman," he says. "I'm not calling those people liars; they saw something. But I go with the scientists who say that some kind of large bird somehow got into the Ohio Valley and decided to stay a few days."

Four days after the initial sighting, the paper published Turner's Page One story quoting Robert L. Smith, associate professor of wildlife biology in West Virginia University's division of forestry, as saying he thought Mothman was a large sandhill crane. Smith theorized the big bird had stopped over at the McClintick Wildlife Station on its way South for the winter.

Could the 'Moth Man' Be Balloon?

POINT PLEASANT, W. Va. (AP) — "He flies through the air with the greatest of ease, with bloodshot eyes and wings as big as you please."

With some poetic license thrown in, that is the description given to the "moth-man," a so-called "winged man" who reportedly has visited an old dynamite dump near here.

Two Point Pleasant couples received the first "visitation" Tuesday night. Mr. and Mrs. Roger Scarberry and Mr. and Mrs. Steve Mallett said they "saw something" at the dump "which made them plenty scared."

The "something" they described as "resembling a flying man . . . between six and seven feet tall. . .with the wings of an angel and penetrating red eyes."

The couples said the "thing" chased them as they drove at speeds up to 100 miles per hour.

Edward Prichard, an advisor to the high school science club at Fairland High School, thinks he has the answer to what the Scarberrys and Malletts saw. Prichard believes the "monster" could be a large gas balloon which the science club released to study prevailing wind currents.

"Light catches these things (balloons) in strange ways at some angles," he said. "Imagination can do the rest."

That Mothman: Would You Believe A Sandhill Crane?

By RALPH TURNER

The case of the Mason County monster may have been solved Friday by a West Virginia University professor.

Dr. Robert L. Smith, associate professor of wildlife biology in WVU's division of forestry, told Mason Sheriff George Johnson at Point Pleasant he believes the "thing" which has been frightening people in the Point Pleasant area since Tuesday is a large bird which stopped off while migrating south.

"From all the descriptions I have read about this 'thing' it perfectly matches the sandhill crane," said the professor. "I definitely believe that's what these people are seeing."

Since Tuesday more than 10 people have spotted what they described as a "birdman" or "mothman" in the area of the McClintick Wildlife Station.

They described it as a huge gray-winged creature with large red eyes.

Dr. Smith said the sandhill crane stands an average of five feet and has gray plumage. A feature of its appearance is a bright red flesh area around each eye. It has an average wing spread of about seven feet.

"Somebody who has never seen anything like it before could easily get the impression it is a flying man," he said. "Car lights would cause the bare skin to reflect as big red circles around the eyes."

While such birds are rare to this area, Dr. Smith said this is migration time and it would not be too difficult for one or more of the birds to stop off at the wildlife refuge. There are no official sightings of such birds in West Virginia, although there have been unconfirmed reports in the past, he added.

The birds are rarely seen east of the Mississippi now except in Florida. Distribution mainly is in Canada and the population is increasing in the Midwest. They winter in Southern California, in Mexico and along the Gulf Coast.

According to one book, the sandhill crane is a "fit successor" to the great whooping crane which is almost extinct. The book states that the height of the male when it stands erect is nearly that of a man of average stature, while the bird's great wings carry its compact and muscular body with perfect ease at a high speed.

Dr. Smith said that while the birds are powerful fliers they cannot match the 100 mph speed one couple reported the "thing" attained when pursuing their car.

Dr. Smith warned that while the sandhill crane is harmless if left alone, that if cornered it may become a formidable antagonist. Its dagger-like bill is a dangerous weapon which the crane does not hesitate to use when at bay and fighting for its life. Many a hunter's dog has been badly injured, he said.

Some of those who reported seeing the "monster" remembered best the eerie sound it made. The description of the sandhill crane also fits there.

"The cry of the sandhill crane is a veritable voice of nature, untamed and unterrified," says one book on birds. "Its uncanny quality is like that of the loon, but is more pronounced because of the much greater volume of the crane's voice. Its resonance is remarkable and its carrying power is increased by a distinct tremolo effect. Often for several minutes after the birds have vanished the unearthly sound drifts back to the listener, like a taunting trumpet from the underworld."

Meanwhile, for the fourth night in a row, an area of the wildlife station again was clogged Friday night with the curious searching for the "thing."

The latest reported sighting came Friday morning from two Point Pleasant volunteer firemen, Captain Paul Yoder and Benjamin Enochs.

"As we were going into the picnic area in the TNT area, Paul and I saw this white shadow go across the car," Mr. Enochs reported.

"This was about 1:30 a.m. Paul stopped the car and I went into the field, but couldn't see anything. I'd say this definitely was a large bird of some kind."

Meanwhile, authorities issued a warning to "monster hunters."

If the "thing" is a migratory crane they had better not shoot it. Migratory birds of all kinds are protected by federal and state wildlife laws.

Sheriff Johnson said he would arrest anybody caught with a loaded gun in the area after dark.

There were earlier reports of armed people in the area.

Sheriff Johnson also warned that the scores of persons searching the abandoned powerhouse in the TNT area after dark risk possible serious injury.

More Sightings
'Birdman' Could Be FHS Balloon

archives
Nov. 18, 1966

A Fairland High School teacher suggested Thursday that the seven-foot "mothman" seen flying the Point Pleasant area Tuesday night and early Wednesday may have been an experimental balloon.

Edward Prichard of Huntington, adviser for the Proctorville, O., school's Science Interest Club, said two balloons were recently released as part of an air current study project.

They were plastic sacks filled with natural gas and measured some four-by-seven feet when inflated, he said. One was released Tuesday night and another Wednesday morning.

A similar balloon was released November 1 and apparently triggered several regional "unidentified flying object" reports before it came to earth near Pruntytown, W.Va. A capsule inside the balloon asks the finder to return it to the school.

Mr. Prichard said the balloons released from the school would be carried over Mason County by prevailing winds "and people's imaginations might do the rest. Besides, the wind can play tricks with these things and they do look strange at times."

One radio station came to Mason County armed and carrying tear gas bombs Wednesday night.

Raymond Wamsley, Mrs. Katherine Wamsley and Mrs. Marcella Bennett visited at the Ralph Thomas home Wednesday, a short distance from the TNT power plant where the "creature" is supposedly domiciled.

Mrs. Bennett, carrying her baby in her arms, started to her car and was suddenly confronted with the "Bird of Paradise." She screamed, and panic-stricken, dropped her baby and fell to the ground. She described the "thing" as a huge, gray winged creature with large red eyes.

Mason Bird-Monster Presumed Gone Now

By RALPH TURNER

POINT PLEASANT — Authorities here have concluded that the so-called Mason County monster was a large bird of some kind and either has been or soon will be frightened out of the McClintic Wildlife Station area by hunters.

It was a week ago today that the first sighting was reported of a large red-eyed winged creature in the McClintic area. Since then there have been about 10 or more similar reports.

The latest report was by four teenaged youths who said they saw a large bird with red eyes fly away from their car at a very high rate of speed. This was 3 a.m. Sunday.

Monday was the first day of open deer hunting season in the McClintic reserve and Chief Deputy Millard Halstead of the Mason County sheriff's office said the influx of hunters undoubtedly would bring any large bird out in the daylight. All "monster" sightings have been at night.

Duane Pursley, wildlife biologist and manager at McClintic, believes small game hunters, which have numbered about 200 a day over McClintic's 2,450 acres, would have flushed any such bird out earlier.

He said he didn't think a large bird, if it did exist, would stay in the area more than a day with all the commotion and hundreds of people searching at night for it.

A West Virginia University wildlife biologist suggested last week that the "thing" is a rare Sandhill Crane.

Mr. Pursley suggested that maybe the "thing", crane, or whatever the people reported seeing, wasn't as large as they thought it was during their excitement.

"We have a lot of Canadian geese stop over here during migration periods, but nothing the size of what these people report," said Mr. Pursley.

He said the hundreds of "thing hunters" had caused a littering and vandalism problem for the wildlife station. He said the area has been littered with cups, cans, bottles and paper and some signs have been damaged.

"There was so much pressure — some people came in here with guns after dark — that we were ready to close off the station area tonight (Monday), but it's eased up and that doesn't appear to be necessary."

Just what was seen in the dark of the night may never be firmly established. The Mason County monster may become a legend. Maybe a new tourist attraction has been born.

BIRD, PLANE OR BATMAN?
Mason Countians Hunt 'Moth Man'

By PAT SILER

POINT PLEASANT — Sightseers clogged the roads north of here Wednesday night as Mason Countians flocked to the desolate TNT area to join in a search for the "Monster Moth Man."

Sheriff's deputies reported that two couples told them that they had sighted the "creature" Tuesday night near the old powerhouse, five miles from Point Pleasant.

It has been variously described as a flying man with a 10-foot wing-spread capable of pursuing cars at 100 miles per hour, and as a huge gray and white bird "with wings like an angel and legs like a man, seven feet tall with two large, red eyes about six inches apart.

Officials at the McClintock Wildlife Station said no such description can be found in any of their fowl manuals. They did suggest, however, that it is geese migrating time, and that flights have been sighted in the area.

But Mr. and Mrs. Robert Scarberry, and Mr. and Mrs. Steve Mallett maintain that the "thing" followed their car Tuesday night, zig-zagging in front of the auto as it speeded along W.Va. 62.

The men told deputies the creature veered away as the car approached the Point Pleasant city limits.

The volunteer fire department was called to assist Wednesday night in traffic duty at the scene of the "flyover."

One fireman commented, "It looks like Mason County fair time."

Owl? Goose? Prank: Or Take Your Choice

Special to the Advertiser

POINT PLEASANT— Telephone calls continued to flood the sheriff's office here today concerning the "creature" which reportedly was slighted flying in the area Tuesday night. Some say they saw it and others tried to explain the apparition.

The latest report was that the "Monster Moth Man" followed a motorist to Cheshire, Ohio, during the early morning hours.

"Despite the confusion, the reports are amusing," a sheriff's deputy said today. The deputy said nearly everyone has voiced an opinion as to what they believed the people actually saw. They included: A large owl, a migrating goose and boys playing pranks with some type of rigged device.

The deputy was asked his opinio "I think it was one of those lar; birds with pencil-like legs and long beak that catches fish — I car think of its name of hand."

Whatever it was, has been variousl described as a flying man with 10-foot wing-spread capable of pu: suing cars at 100 miles an hour, an as a huge gray and white bird wit wings like an angel and legs like man, seven feet tall with two larg red eyes about six inches apart.

Sightseers clogged roads nort of here Wednesday night trying fo a glimpse of the "monster" and t join in a search for him or it.

The fire department was calle out to assist in traffic duty along Route 62 near the old TNT plant.

This page, top photo: *An extremely rare photograph of an impromptu press conference held by the Mason County Sheriff's Department the day after the November 15, 1966 Mothman sightings. In the center on the phone is Deputy Alva Sullivan, along with two unidentified deputies.*

Next page, top left and right photos: *Original Mothman witness Linda Scarberry (interviewed in* Mothman: Facts Behind the Legend*), shown in her senior picture and later in the mid-70s in a photo published in a national tabloid.*

Next page, bottom: *Mothman as drawn by an original eyewitness just hours after the encounter.*

LINDA Scarberry ... the first person to see Mothman.

One of the few photos in existence of the black '57 Chevy that the two couples rode in on Tuesday, November 15, 1966. The creature chased the terrified occupants from the TNT area down Route 62 into the Point Pleasant city limits. Only hours later, the Mason County Sheriff's Department began its investigation of the first of many sightings of the winged, bird-like creature. (Photo courtesy of Linda Scarberry)

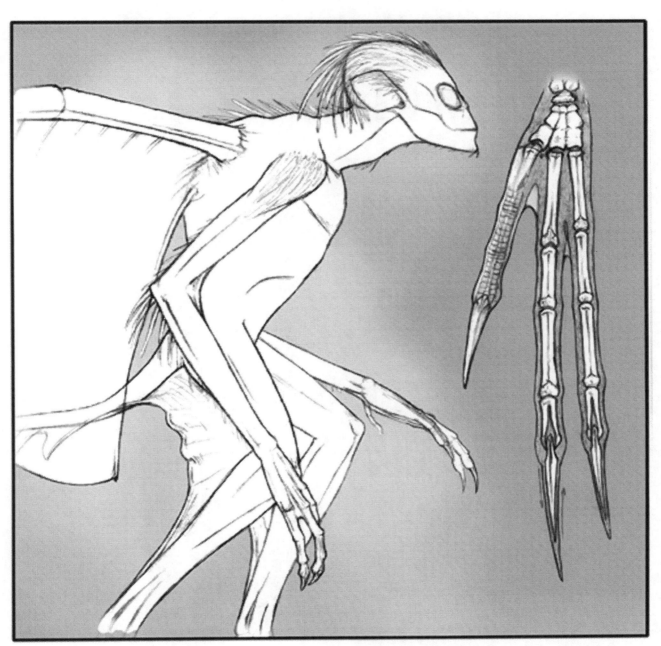

Illustration by Natalie "Orbyss" Grewe

Illustration by Gary Gibeaut

```
Case Number: WV-35559-102M
WITNESS NAME: MERLE PARTRIDGE

Sighting Report: Centerpoint/Salem WV
Description: Rotating Red Lights at Home
Report Date: November 14, 1966
```

Where's My Bandit???

Back in the 1980s, when my rock band buddies and I played the bar circuit in New Martinsville, West Virginia, at a little club there called the Pink Panther (another book in itself), the drive to Centerpoint, West Virginia, was a long one, longer than it seemed in reality. A long drive back then seemed like nothing, but this time the anticipation grew stronger as I passed through one small river town after the other. I was on my way to interview Merle Partridge about his German shepherd Bandit that disappeared and was never found on the evening of November 14, 1966.

The following night the Mothman sightings began to take place in Point Pleasant at the North Power Plant in the TNT area. Were these two events somehow related? Mr. Partridge lived with his family in Centerpoint, which sits about two hours driving time north of Point Pleasant. When I finally arrived at Merle's house, I was greeted by a very small, black Chihuahua who seemed bent on scaring me off. I joked with Merle and asked him if this was Bandit.

When Mr. Partridge's story was originally investigated in 1966 by author and UFO investigator Gray Barker from nearby Clarksburg, his name was listed as Newell Partridge. When speaking to Merle on the phone just a few weeks before my interview, he explained to me that when he was four years old his birth certificate was mistakenly listed as Newell instead of his real first name, Merle. Both John Keel's book, as well as Gray Barker's book, have the name Newell Partridge in them, partly because Barker shared some of his investigative information with Mr. Keel at that time.

You were living in Salem, West Virginia, when all of this happened?

We lived in Centerpoint, West Virginia, which is in between Salem and Clarksburg. We lived on Pike Fork. I had a farm there with around 115 acres.

How did your encounter end up in John Keel's book? Was it because you had spoken to Gray Barker? Did you report what happened to you to the authorities?

Pete Lymon was at WBOY-TV in Clarksburg at the time. I knew him pretty well. I was in the construction business and I would call him occasionally for weather reports, and since I had a construction company, I did some advertising on the station.

How far was Clarksburg from where you lived?

About twenty miles. After all of this happened, the next day I spoke to Pete and he mentioned something like, "Well, you had some kind of experience out there, didn't you?" I told him what had happened. The day after, a whole group of people came out to our house. There was an Air Force colonel, a detective, and a few others.

So word had spread fairly quickly after your encounter?

Yes, it did.

Did you want to speak about it or did you want to keep quiet about it?

No…we did not want these people there. My wife still will hardly talk to anyone about it, because we received phone calls for years after this had happened. People would call up and say things like "cuckoo" over the phone.

So all of your children were present at the time of your sighting?

Oh yeah…they were all at home. The whole family was in the house.

Did the people who came to investigate your story sit you down and ask you a lot of questions?

Well, this one man was in plainclothes. He asked me to stand out in the field and point down in the direction of where I saw the lights. My wife told him to go to hell, and that I was not going to stand out there like some "dumb hillbilly" and point to an empty field. She ran them off. She got pretty uptight about it and I can't blame her. But it was a very spooky thing that had happened.

Did your wife see the lights also?

Oh, yeah…certainly.

So these people just wanted to know what you had witnessed?

But you see, there are so many other things that are tied into this. There are a few days after this that another incident happened that involved another man and his two young sons. In fact, I ran into one of those boys about two or three years ago.

So did these people see the same thing?

They saw something that resembled the same thing that I saw, but this goes into a whole new story: about how this boy's father had panicked, and how he came to our house very late one night, pounding on the front door, claiming that his son was missing. He could not find his youngest son…he had his oldest son with him. He had wrecked his car in a ditch just down the road from our house. He needed help, so when we went up to pull his car out of the ditch, his missing son came walking up the road from the other direction.

He would have had to walk ten miles around the entire hill to get to where he was walking.

When I ran into the youngest son a few years, back he asked me if I knew who he was, and I told him I didn't know who he was. He said, "I am the youngest son who was lost that night back in '66." I told him I was glad to see him, and I asked him what really happened that night. He said, "I don't know…I have no recollection at all as to what happened."

Did the people investigating your encounter come out after the first visit to ask more questions?

They came just that one time, and then Gray Barker came out maybe a week later. If Gray Barker wrote the entire story in his book *The Silver Bridge*, he got some of stuff screwed up…that's not actually the way it happened.

Do you remember what time in the evening you began to notice something strange was happening at your house?

About 11 o'clock at night.

Can you describe to me what exactly happened?

My wife and I were sitting, watching television. I remember we watching a TV show that had a poodle in it named Misieur Cognac. I can't tell you the name of the movie, but it was a white French poodle. All at once the television set started winding up like a high pitched generator, like one of the old army-style generators that you used to hand crank. It wound up to a fever pitch. At the same time our dog Bandit was on the front porch, letting out these long death howls (describes how the howls sounded)….

Bandit was a full grown German Shepherd?

Yes…he weighed about 110 lbs…fairly big sized dog. As the television was winding up, I was trying to figure out what was going on, and I got up to go over and turn it down, because it was hurting our ears because of the way it was screaming. Then the whole picture tube and everything just blew out into the middle of the floor. Glass went everywhere. By that time, Bandit was carrying on so I ran out onto the front porch. As I ran out Bandit took off down through the field.

Well, the only thing that was in that field was a little pump house. I looked down to where he was running, and yelled for him to come back. That dog always obeyed me, but this time he wouldn't mind me at all. When I looked down there, all I could see were red lights going around. They were not eyes or anything like that. They were intermittent red lights.

So you did not see any type of red eyes of any type?

No. This thing disappeared after only a few minutes. The first thing that entered my mind was that it was a helicopter…but there was no noise. I stood outside and called the dog for a bit, and then went back in the house, more or less just trying to put it out my mind as something weird. My wife was sweeping up the glass from the television. We then went to bed. I can't say what happened was not out of the ordinary, because it was. I was like anybody and lay in bed thinking, *What in the hell was that? I had never seen anything like this before.*

The next morning I got up and I went down there. You could see the dog tracks going down through the wet grass. You could see the dog's path. When I got down there, you could see these dog tracks all around this huge circle of mashed down grass. The circle was about 40 or 50 feet in diameter. That is when I started thinking, *There had been something here besides a helicopter.* I remember coming back to the house and telling my wife that the dog was gone.

Did you contact anyone at this point about what you had seen?

I remember talking to someone about the dog being missing…I hated my dog being gone. I wanted people to keep an eye out for it, or maybe run an ad in the newspapers or something. That is when I heard on a radio news report that a state trooper had seen some kind of a big, bird-like creature standing alongside of a highway, holding the carcass of a large dog. I put two and two together, then…*that's my dog, I'll bet.*

I called a boy who worked for me up on the phone, and asked him if he could come over. I told him that I wanted to show him something. He lived about two miles from me, and before I could finish my sentence, he said he had something to show me as well.

When he arrived, I said, "You know what happened to my TV last night? The whole damn thing blew out into the middle of the floor." He looked at me and said, "no kidding…what do you think I came over to tell *you*?"

He said, "Mine did the same thing at about 11 o'clock last night." So then I am really starting to think. I began to tell him what had happened, and we both decided to scout around and try to maybe find something. We were really spooked at that time and starting to get more scared as the days went by. Another thing that was weird about all of this was, that the beginning of the day after this happened, there was no sound anywhere of anything. There were no wildlife sounds around there at all. You didn't hear a cricket…you didn't hear a bird…you didn't hear a cow moo…you didn't hear anything! It was absolutely dead silence.

> POINT PLEASANT, W. Va. (UPI)—Eight people say they saw a flying creature near this Ohio River community, a dog could have fallen victim to "it," and now a Kanawha County gravedigger saw a "brown man" fly past him last weekend.
>
> Kenneth Duncan of Blue Creek near Charleston said he and some other men were digging his brother-in-law's grave on Saturday when something that "looked like a brown human being" buzzed past.
>
> "It was gliding through the trees and was in sight for about a minute," Duncan said. Four other men helping to dig the grave didn't see it.
>
> The "thing," described as a huge bird-like creature with eyes like "red reflectors" and a wing span of 10 feet, first was reported to police by Steve Mallette and Roger Scarberry and their wives who said they saw it three times late Tuesday and early Wednesday about five miles north of here.
>
> Four other persons also told Mason County Sheriff George Johnson they saw it in the same general area.
>
> And a contractor, Newell Partridge, who lives 100 miles to the north, said he feels it may have had something to do with the disappearance of his $350 German shepherd dog, Bandit.
>
> Partridge said he sighted the "thing" in a meadow near his home in Doddridge County about 90 minutes before the Point Pleasant sightings.
>
> Partridge said his television set "began acting like a generator" and Bandit "started carrying on something terrible."
>
> Partridge said he shined a flashlight into the field and saw something with eyes like "red reflectors." The dog's hair stood straight up, he said, and the animal went into the field.
>
> The dog never returned, Partridge said, and there was no trace of it in the morning.
>
> Johnson said he was not discounting the stories he was told but said he feels what was seen was nothing more than a "freak shitepoke," a large bird of the heron family.
>
> The shitepoke, sometimes called a shag, is the smallest heron in the Western Hemisphere. Officials were at a loss, however, to explain how a shag could fly at 100 miles per hour as Scarberry and Mallette said the creature did.

How long did this silence last?

It lasted about a week. Then about a week later another weird incident took place at the house. We were sitting watching TV again (a new TV set had been purchased to replace the blown one) and by this time, I am sitting with a gun right beside of my chair, because we are way out in the middle of nowhere with no houses within a mile.

All of a sudden, someone hits my front porch banging on the door. The man was hollering, "I need help!" I yelled back, "Who is it?" He then replied again, "I need help!" I said, "You're going to need a helluva lot of help in about a half a second because I am fixing to blow that door of its hinges". He then yelled, "I need help...my kid is missing...my kid is missing!"

So I opened the door, with the gun in my hand, because I was still skeptical at this point. The man told me he was coming down the hill about a half a mile from my house, and as he started to come around the turn at the bottom of the hill, something took off beside the road, right beside his car. He said there were lights flashing and there was no noise. He said it vanished almost as fast as they had seen it. He said it was big and moved very quickly. He had his one son with him but told me his youngest son was missing and that they could not find him.

His car was in the ditch and he had ran down to our house. I told him we could take my jeep and pull his car out of the ditch, and see if we could find his boy and maybe he was there waiting on them. So I took my jeep pickup with chains in the back, and we went to where his car was in the ditch. I pulled the car out of the ditch, and told the man to drive down to our house, and he could call the police, so we can get them out looking for his young boy.

When we started to head back to our house, we looked down the road about 200 yards, and saw the young boy walking up the road towards us from the other direction. His father ran and grabbed him, asking him where he had been, and the boy could hardly talk or answer him. He couldn't remember anything about what had happened.

Later that following summer, my wife and my kids were all out in our backyard, where I had put a swimming pool in. We were all just laying on the deck looking up. All at once that whole sky just blacked out.

This thing that we saw was so immense that I couldn't even begin to tell you how big it was. If you were to ask me how big it was, I would say it was 10 miles long and 10 miles long the other way, because it was so humongous that was all you could see...there was nothing else. It was a mechanical object.

I have been around enough to know something mechanical from something that is spiritual. No noise, it had portals, I was just flabbergasted. I asked my kids if they were seeing what I was seeing, and they said, "Yes...what is it?...what is it?" I said, "It's a damn hotel, I think!" Just as quick as it appeared it was gone. Seeing that would make a believer out of anyone.

Do you believe that maybe the Air force or military had anything to do with these objects that you saw?

> The "thing," which has been described by clever writers and newscasters throughout the country as a "monster moth," "red-eyed demon" and "bird-man," was spotted near here about 90 minutes after the Doddridge County dog disappeared.
>
> Patridge said his flashlight picked up "two red reflections" in his meadow and at this the dog's hair stood up, he bared his teeth and rushed into the woods.
>
> Doddridge County is approximately 60 miles from here — as the "bird" flies. And the local couples said the creature they saw traveled about 100 miles an hour.
>
> Officials at McClintic today

No I don't, because this thing was so big that if it had been under development by the military, we would have sure known about it by now.

Going back to Bandit the dog, do you recall what the weather conditions were the night the dog disappeared?

It was a very clear, cold night. What I saw behind our house was mechanical. It was not spiritual, and it was not wildlife of any type. The lights seemed to be intermittent and moved in a circular motion. When you see something like that at 11 or 12 o'clock at night, and you are out in the country in the middle of nowhere, I don't know if your mind really wants to think of what you are seeing.

What were the circulating red lights seen behind the Partridge home that night? I must admit, I was expecting to hear of an encounter describing the two, eerie red eyes. These always seems to be the common denominator in almost all of the Mothman descriptions I have read about or investigated myself. On several occasions during my conversation, Merle emphasized to me that he saw "mechanical" red lights flashing intermittently, and not two distinct red eyes. I find it interesting how his story was thrust into the Mothman media attention, just for the simple fact that he thought that the large dead dog found in Point Pleasant only days later could have been his missing dog Bandit.

I have spoken to some of the witnesses in Point Pleasant, but as of yet, no one has ever been able to confirm what the dead dog looked like. Mothman witness Linda Scarberry told me that the dog was found near the C.C. Lewis farm, just on the outskirts of Point Pleasant, only a few miles south of the TNT area. Previous books and recorded accounts have always stated that Merle had reported seeing something with red eyes, but no flashing lights of any type were mentioned.

Whatever happened to Bandit will always remain a mystery, but it is no mystery that many people were scared to venture out of their homes for fear of what might be flying in the skies above them. One resident of Point Pleasant told me that children were not allowed to have recess outdoors at several of the local grade schools during this time, because parents and school officials were afraid that a child on the playground might be harmed — or possibly even be picked up off of the ground — by what locals were reporting as a "larger than normal bird."

Merle explained that he felt that the unexplained occurrences that took place at his home and to him, even months and years later, maybe were somehow all intertwined and related. One experience he told me about occured while driving his tractor trailer truck cross country from California up into Canada a few years later. While driving his truck in Canada, he was involved in a traffic accident that resulted in the death of a 16 year old girl; another motorist had caused the wreck by trying to run a red light, causing Merle's truck to hit the other car.

Even though Merle was not at fault, he still expressed feeling bad about the whole incident, but went on with his normal trucking routine, delivering truckloads of fruit and other goods literally all over the country. There came a time where he had to make a delivery to the same area where the accident had occurred, so in order to avoid bad memories of the accident, he decided to take an alternative route and bypass the scene of the accident all together. While driving parallel, but miles away on a completely different highway, he said the cab of his truck began to glow bluish in color and that all the electronic gear and components suddenly began to blow.

The battery near the engine completely split in half, and after nearly $700 in electronic repairs, he began his journey towards home. He could never pin down the cause of all the strange power surges, and to this day believes that it is related to the accident years prior to this experience.

On one other occasion, he said he had pulled over alongside the interstate, down South, to get some sleep in his truck cab. He explained that during those days, he and most truckers depended on a good night's rest, instead of pills or caffeine, to help keep them awake and that it was always better to be safe than to be sorry. In the early morning hours he awoke, only to find himself covered in a tangled mess of cobwebs. He immediately thought that the cobwebs had come form the fresh load of lettuce that he hauling from California, but was still baffled as to how that large of an amount had ended up in his cab and all over him.

After cleaning his cab (and himself!) of the cobwebs, he began to head towards his delivery destination, only to discover that another truck driver parked near his truck on the freeway had been shot to death while asleep in his cab. Merle couldn't help but think this was just another verse in another chapter of unexplainable events that he and his family experienced.

A mysterious "mechanical" object with flashing "red" lights, the unexplained disappearance of a full-grown German shepherd dog, the young boy who couldn't remember why he was lost, and the chilling events that happened while driving his tractor trailer, all seem to play a part in the bigger picture of things I encounter, researching what some of these people such as Merle Partridge were experiencing during the 1960s…possibly even today.

ARCHIVES:
The TNT Area Power Plants

An aerial photograph looking south over the TNT area, with the Power Plants circled (North Power Plant in the left, lower circle, and the South Power Plant.) Fairground Road, running top-to-bottom between each plant, was popular for drag racing in the 1960s.

The abandoned North Power Plant prior to being demolished in the early 1990s.

A rare photo of the South Power Plant prior to its implosion.

An aerial view of the South Power Plant. Note massive pond area located in front of the structure, later filled in.

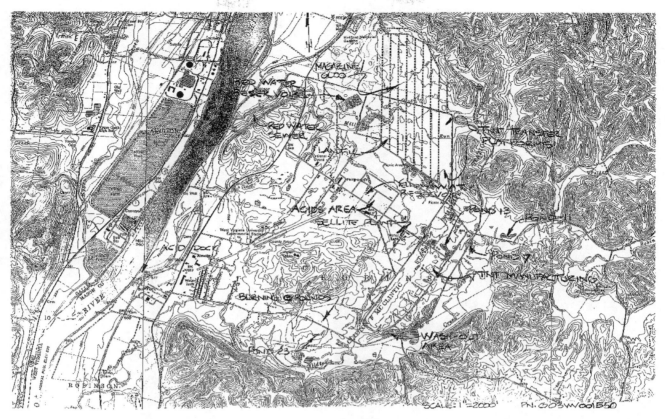

This grainy topographical map shows the production areas of the former TNT plant. Note parallel grid of roads which run among the concrete igloos at top center of map.

This recent photo of an igloo shows the entrance doors to the domed structure. The igloos were utilized for storage of explosives even long after the war effort.

Following pages: *The implosion of the South Power Plant is captured in these time-lapse photos taken at the moment of demoliton in the early 1990s.*

Illustration by Cardboard Midget

Case Number: WV-35559-103M
WITNESS NAME: SHIRLEY HENSLEY

Sighting Report: Huntington, WV
Description: Red-Eyed Creature
Report Date: Early 1960s

That Red-Eyed Monster

When I first sat down with Shirley Hensley, I could see the apprehension in her eyes as she began to tell me what she and her family experienced at their home just on the outskirts of Huntington, West Virginia, in the early 1960s. Huntington is a much larger town than Point Pleasant, but is only about an hour's drive away. It was years later that Shirley began to rethink the details of seeing what her family referred to as the "red eyed monster," and wondered, in the back of her mind, if these encounters could somehow be related to the Mothman sightings in nearby Point Pleasant. It was obvious to me that Shirley was feeling a little uneasy talking about the subject, as she explained to me that the few people she and her family had confided in over the years had either laughed it off — or called them all crazy. One late night, her father took a shot at the figure near the family's coal pile with a .22 caliber rifle as they watched it scramble and scurry up the hillside into the night. For years Shirley's father told the story of "two big, red eyes" peering over the pile of coal.

Can you remember the year and time span that all of this happened?

It was around 1961 and continued through 1964. I was married in 1964 and then Mom and Dad moved away from there.

Where was your house located?

This was on what they used to call 31st Street hill, but the real name was Crotty street. Located right up over the hill behind our house was Rotary Park.

So you were not out in the countryside very far?

No. My family was very poor, and I didn't realize that other people did not live the way that we did. We had an outhouse, and burnt wood and coal for heat, and basically lived in a shack. We existed from day to day. I am the oldest of nine children, and when something like this happens, it is just part of the misery and you just think that it is just another part of your life. We felt fortunate if a lot of time would pass before we heard this thing again. We not only could hear it, but it went around the house and it would bump up against the side of the house.

We had plastic covering the windows instead of real glass windows. There was one very big window, and whatever this thing was, could have just come right through it if it had wanted to. You could hear the grunting noise as it bumped up against the house and the leaves crackling under its feet. We could also hear a gargling type of sound, and then a very loud scream would come out...and it was a blood-curdling scream like nothing I had ever heard before or since.

Since your family lived on the outskirts of the city, almost into the country, do you feel that maybe there could have been coyotes or animals like that possibly on the hills behind your house?

I don't know what was up in the hills in Rotary Park. People back in those days thought of coyotes as being mainly out west.

Did you or your family ever hear any noise coming from atop your roof at any time?

No, we did not. You are the first person who has ever asked me that. It just went around the house. Our water well was just out the road from our house, and we would have to go out with a bucket and drop it down in the well and get our water for the next morning. We all took turns getting the water, and we had a rule that we had to get the water in before dark — that is when this thing always came around. We never saw it in the daylight, so everyone knew that they had to bring in the water before dark. If you didn't do it then it didn't get done.

Illustration by Steven Ring

How often did you hear this noise outside your house: was it just a few times, or over a few years?

No. When it started, it would come around one or two nights for about three weeks, and then it would go away. This went on for about three years.

What was your father's reaction when the noise started outside?

At first, my parents had other things on their mind other than this stuff that they called foolishness. The first time I ever heard it was near an old flatbed truck that sat out in the road in front of our house. I had a boyfriend who would visit me at that time, and I was so ashamed of our house so we would sit in the cab of that truck and talk. We were sitting in the truck and we heard something bump up against the truck from underneath, and a loud scream. At first I thought it was one of our neighbor's pigs making the noise. I found out later that he did not have any pigs. We finally jumped out of the truck and ran into the house.

Illustration by Shawn Kennedy

A few days later my mother and I, along with a couple of my brothers and sisters, went to the well to get some water. Behind the well were some large bushes and tress. When she dropped the bucket in the well, we heard that familiar scream coming from the area where the bushes were. She grabbed us and told us all to run to the house. That was the first time my mother heard it.

Can you tell me what happened when your father shot at it ?

I remember it was in the fall, because I was dating my husband at that time, and my father told me I had to be home by dark, so I would always be home by about 6pm. I had just walked up our driveway and opened the front door, and my mother ran into the room. She was frantic and told me to get in the house, because they had heard that thing again. She said that my father had gone out to get my other two sisters who were outside playing. Dad said he had heard it scream, and after pushing my two sisters into the house, he hunkered down by the door.

Just out from our front porch was our neighbor's coal pile. He said he could hear it scrambling in the coal pile, so he stuck his arm in our door and told our neighbor Delmer to hand him a gun. Delmer's son handed dad out a .22 rifle. Dad always hated the fact that it was only a .22 and that it couldn't do much damage — if in fact he did get a good shot at it. He pulled the gun up to shoot, and as he watched, he could see two large, red eyes coming up over the coal. He shot at it, and it let out a loud scream and started running towards the hill.

How did he describe its features such as body size and color?

Dad was a little angry, because he had told my sister Mary to stay in the house, but she had witnessed the whole thing while standing behind him. She said it was a big, tall,

black shiny thing with big red eyes. Dad described it as at least 7 feet tall, and that it had very long arms that went down past its knees and that when it ran up the hillside the arms stayed down at its side. He said it ran in an awkward manner.

Did the scream that you heard resemble any type of animal or bird?

No, because my dad grew up in Fayette county years ago. People had tried to tell him that what we hearing and seeing was a panther, but dad always said that a panther either screams like a woman or sounds like a baby crying. He said it was neither of those. He also dismissed it as being a screech owl of any sort.

My two sisters would look for footprints or tracks and one day they found a big print in the dirt. Dad came out and looked at it, and said he had never seen any tracks that resembled that type of footprint before.

I was always amazed at the fact that whatever this thing was never hurt anyone. I think that it was as afraid of us as we were afraid of it. We had these two little hound dogs named Roscoe and Sluggo, and they stayed outside because we didn't keep dogs in the house. When we would hear this thing scream the dogs would just come tearing at the door wimpering and terror stricken. When we would open the door and let them in, the hair on their back would be literally standing straight up in the air. They would claw to get under the covers on the bed and just sit there and shake.

How did your father describe the eyes when he shot at it that night?

He said they looked like red bicycle reflectors.

Shirley went on the tell me that she and her immediate neighbors at that time still get together to discuss the unexplained "red eyed monster" that roamed the hillside around their houses near Huntington. It was during 1966 when she heard about the weird sightings of a large bird with red eyes in Point Pleasant; this is when she began to wonder if the incidents were related.

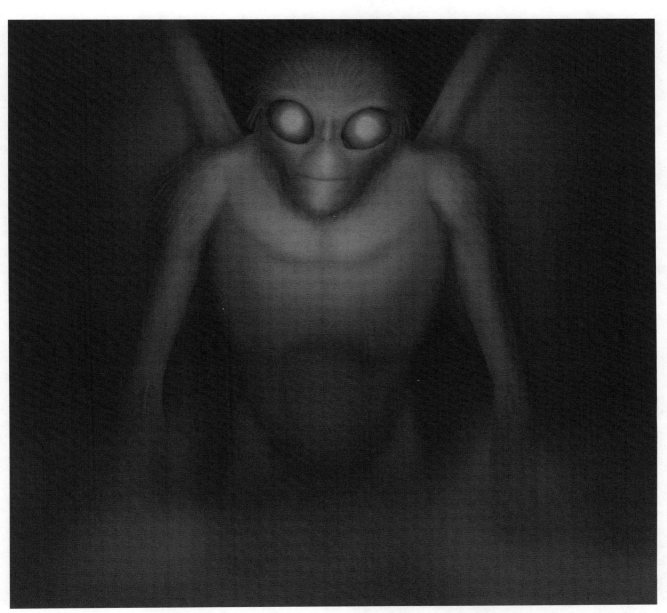

Illustration by Natalie "Orbyss" Grewe

Illustration by Gary Gibeaut

Case Number: WV-35559-104M
WITNESS NAME: MARCELLA BENNETT

Sighting Report: Sister's Home/TNT Area
Description: Large Winged Creature
Report Date: November 16, 1966

Face to Face with Mothman

The night after Linda Scarberry and others encountered a large, winged creature in the TNT area Marcella Bennett and her brother and sister-in-law decided to pay a visit to family members who lived in the general vicinity of TNT. The very last thing on Marcella's mind was to come face to face with the same terrifying creature the others had spotted the night before. It was Wednesday, November 16th and what started off as a typical drive to visit relatives turned into a night Marcella has never forgotten. Marcella may very well be one of the rarest of Mothman witnesses who literally stared the creature in the face while attempting to run for safety and protect her tiny daughter at the same time. Her story is chilling and direct in its delivery and Marcella makes no reservations about what she saw that November night.

Marcella Bennett's story is one of high priority for many who are interested in the Mothman investigations because of her specific descriptions and details describing the six foot figure that rose up beside of her car almost as if it had been waiting on her and her small child. Her story remains to this day the same as it was in 1966 and undoubtedly is one of the most intriguing and horrific accounts of staring directly into the face of a tall, birdlike creature that many have called the Mothman.

Illustration by Aric Slater

When your encounter took place on November 16, 1966, were you aware of the sighting by Linda Scarberry and the others on the previous night of November 15th?

My sister and her husband lived up there around the TNT area. We had stopped by my mother's house in Henderson, and had picked up the newspaper and read about it. We thought it would be fun to drive up there and maybe spook the children at my sister's house, but my sister and her husband had gone to church. So my brother Raymond, and his wife Cathy and I, all decided to drive up and visit awhile with the kids. When we arrived there, only the three kids were at the house.

When we went in, we asked them about what people were seeing up in the TNT area, and if they were afraid being there by themselves. They said no, so we stayed for awhile and then we decided to leave around 9 pm before my sister and her husband had returned. When we started out the door to leave, my brother Raymond stopped when he got down towards the bottom of the steps.

Was he in front of you or behind you?

He and his wife Cathy were walking in front of me. He stopped and was trying to get my attention as I walked past them and walked towards the car. He said, "Look up in the sky to your right Marcella...what is that in the sky, coming?" At that point, I was not really interested or paying much attention and I continued to walk towards the car. I was carrying my two-year-old daughter Tina in my arms. I was driving that evening, so I had the car keys in my hand. I just kept ignoring my bother Raymond, but I turned and when I did, I saw the light. Raymond yelled, "It's not a plane, but what is it?" I said, "I don't know," but at that point...it was like I wasn't in control of listening to my brother trying to stop me to see this light in the sky. I saw the light. but at the same time, it was almost like I was being drawn to go on towards the car.

How far was the car from the house?

It was a short distance out, because we hadn't pulled right up to the house, probably about twenty yards. So I just kept walking, and Raymond kept yelling, "Stop! Look at this light! What is it?" It was just like a magnet pulling me towards the car, and I didn't feel like I was in control of myself.

Can you describe the lights that you saw?

They were real brilliant lights, almost as if they would hurt your eyes to stare directly at them. I know what a plane looks like. and it wasn't a plane's lights. When I got to the car, I had my daughter Tina in my right arm and the car keys in the other hand. I was the driver that evening, but for some reason, I went to the passenger side of the car. When I started to unlock the car door, I remember looking down at the car keys, and I saw these legs that looked like gray feathers. They looked like a man's legs, but I did not see feet. I just started looking up towards the body, and when I looked at the shoulders and head, I could see that this thing wasn't a man. It looked more like a bird, but in my mind I knew it was too big to be a bird.

The head was stuck down in the shoulder area and hung over, and the shoulders were almost in an upward position (demonstrates body posture). My immediate reaction was that I had never seen anything like this before and my mind was racing. I was paralyzed and could not move at this point. I just stood there and looked at it, but I couldn't figure out what it was that I was seeing.

How close were you standing to it?

Within a few feet. It just rose up, and stood as if it were just relaxing up against the side of the car. I just thought my life was over. This was something I had never seen or heard tell of before, even in my wildest imagination. I just couldn't figure out what I was looking at, but I knew it wasn't a man. It did look like a big bird, because its arms were like wings.

Were the wings extended?

The wings were drawn in towards its body, and its head was sunken down in the shoulders like a bird. Its head was tilted sideways.

Did you see any type of red eyes?

I did not see any red eyes. I have never said that I had seen red eyes. I don't know if I was too frightened to even notice any type of red eyes at that time.

Do you recall any type of facial features?

No. I do know that there was a head. At first I thought I was seeing gray, khaki clothes, but then I realized that it was not clothing, but looked more like feathers. I was in the dark but I was very close to it.

Did it make any sounds at all?

It did not make any sounds at all. I just figured my time is over, and I'm going to die. I

thought that at any moment this thing was going to either pick me up or hurt my little girl. I could hear my brother yelling at this point.

Did your brother see it?

He saw it but he would not come towards where we were. He and his wife were both very frightened. He kept yelling, "Marcella! Run! Run!" I tried to turn my body to run and I couldn't because it just like I was frozen.

Many people that I have talked to have described an "indescribable feeling of fear" during their experiences. It's as if they almost had a sixth sense that was warning them of something about to happen.

Well, it's like me telling my brother, who kept telling me to look up and look at that bright light. I knew it was an unusual light, and I had never seen anything as bright, but it was almost as if I were hypnotized or drawn into walking towards the car. But I could hear him yelling to me, "Stop, stop, come back!" And it still rings in my ears today. When I finally got myself turned around, I tried to run towards the house, but I couldn't run. I fell on top of Tina. I could hear her crying but I couldn't get moved off the top of her. I thought that thing was going to pick me up by the back, but I was worried about suffocating her. I just couldn't do what my mind was wanting me to do.

At that point did it make any movements of any kind?

I heard the flapping of wings in the background as I tried to run. It was then that I thought of claws maybe reaching and grabbing me by the back. I had only taken maybe four steps when I fell flat on top of Tina.

Did your brother and his wife run into the house, or did they wait on you until you could make in back to the house?

They were both at the steps waiting. When I did get back to the house I had burnt my hand because I had also been holding a cigarette and my knees were all bleeding and skinned up pretty bad. The side of my face was bleeding from where I had fallen.

What was the overall atmosphere inside of the house at that point?

The children were frightened to death and screaming. No one knew what was going on and they were all hysterical. I can remember hearing my brother calling the Mason County sheriff's department. By that time I was lying on a sofa, and just coming and going while everyone was trying to comfort me. They were wiping the blood off me from where I had fallen.

Had anyone noticed if this thing was still outside of the house?

When Raymond had come in, he locked the front door behind us. I can still hear him telling the sheriff's department to get to TNT area because we had seen this creature. He told them that we were locked in the house, but that it was still outside. Raymond said that when I had got to him at the bottom of the steps, he heard what the flapping of wings as if it were a plane taking off. He heard the wings and that it didn't go very far, but he didn't see it fly because we all had our backs to it. He kept saying that it was still by the house.

Did it come onto the porch of the house?

It came to the front window and looked in the window. I was so distraught by that time that I did not pay much attention, but Raymond saw it. It also came to the front door and sort of shoved on the door. Then the sheriff's deputies arrived, and the front yard was full of police cars.

Illustration by Gary Gibeaut

How long did it take the police to arrive at the house?

I would say not any longer than 15 or 20 minutes. They were there pretty fast. They had heard the same story from the night before, and they were looking all around the house. They did not make a mockery of what we had reported, because they saw that I was injured. They believed what we were telling them, and had guns drawn and were out searching around the house. Before we realized it, the front yard was full of people and cars from everywhere. It looked like a drive-in theater. Raymond talked to the police and filled out the paperwork and police reports.

Did anyone find any type of evidence around the house of this thing's presence?

John Keel was in town at that time, and he and I went back up there a few days later, and found what we thought were footprints of some sort.

Were you visited by the press soon after?

Oh, yes. That first night I made Raymond go home with me, and I told my husband what had happened and what we had saw. He told me to try and calm down and relax, but I could hardly sleep. I would no sooner fall asleep and I would think I could hear the wings flapping and noise on top of the roof. I kept feeling that this thing had followed us home.

Linda Scarberry has stated almost that exact feeling.

I know this sounds like a very strange thing, but this is real and it happened. I am 65 years old and I have never changed my story. I know what I saw, and I know what I heard. I never drove at night after all this happened. One night I had to pick up my husband at work late at night. When I did, I got about halfway there and I felt the presence of whatever that was in the back seat of that car, and I almost wrecked the car that night. I hit the brakes so hard that I jerked my neck and turned around to see if that thing was in the back.

So the experience definitely changed your life?

Yes. I went to Holzer Hospital after about four or five days had passed, because I couldn't sleep, and I was hearing things and thought that it was right outside and still after me. I couldn't imagine what this thing was, or where it came from, and what was its purpose. It was close enough to harm me, but it didn't.

There is no man that looks like what I saw. If there is, then it's from another world because it's nothing I have ever seen in a movie or in my wildest imagination. I have watched a lot of monster movies with creatures and so forth, but this was something that I have never seen anything to resemble.

What is your opinion on the Sandhill Crane theory? Many people were saying that all you and others were seeing was just a stork-like bird.

Oh, that's not what this thing was. I know what a Sandhill Crane looks like (laughs). I've seen many of those. This wasn't a Sandhill Crane — believe me. I know what they look like. I thought that they were way off base. A Sandhill Crane doesn't stand 6 feet tall and have man-like features, and I was close enough to it to know the difference. I know what I saw and I will never change my story.

Illustration by Gary Gibeaut

Were you treated for shock after the encounter?

I was treated for shock two days later when I went to Holzer Hospital. I did not want to tell the doctor what I had seen, but he asked me if I was Marcella Bennett. He asked me if I was one of the people who seen the big bird in Point Pleasant.

So even days and months after your experience, people were still seeing this thing in TNT?

Oh yes, and hunting it with guns and shotguns. There were thousands of cars going in and out of TNT area every night. I went back to TNT maybe a month later, and drove past the North Power Plant and said, "This is it!" — and never went back up there.

Did you know John Keel and Mary Hyre very well?

John Keel and Mary Hyre would visit me and the other witnesses, and we would all take turns meeting at different homes to discuss our experiences and what we had seen. We would take car rides, hoping to see more lights or some connection to what we were experiencing. John was amazed, as we were, about the whole thing and knew we were too upset not to have seen something. He knew we were telling the truth. Mary was a very wonderful lady and I sometimes wonder about her passing at such an early age.

Did you ever have any visits or encounters with the so-called Men in Black?

No I never had any visits from any Men in Black, but I did have strange phone calls. Once when I had went to Columbus, Ohio, all of the clippings and paperwork that I had kept about the Mothman and the UFO activity disappeared from my home. This was only a year after all of the sightings. I had saved and documented every clipping and newspaper mention of the story, and how those disappeared is still a mystery to me to this day.

Do you have any thought on the Silver Bridge collapse and a connection between that disaster and all of the UFO and Mothman activity?

My uncle Robert told me before he passed away to not let people think that I didn't see what I really saw. He lived in an apartment on Main Street, in downtown Point Pleasant, overlooking the Ohio River and right next to the Silver Bridge. He told me that before the bridge fell that he saw what I saw, a man that looked like a bird, and that it went over the bridge.

He has been deceased for about four years now, and he told me to always believe what I saw. Uncle Robert would not ever have told me something like this, and he wanted to make sure that I would stand by my story, which I always have. Every time my husband and I drove over that bridge, I would tell him that was something wrong with that bridge, because it shook so much.

Bob would try to explain to me that the Silver Bridge was a suspension bridge, and that it had to move some or that it would fall. I would tell him that that bridge was going to fall and to hurry up and get across it. I remember feeling the vibration and shaking as we were driving across it earlier on the day it collapsed. The bridge fell at about 5 pm and we had gone over it at noon that day.

What do you have to say to someone who doubts your story or laughs at the thought of a giant bird-like creature?

Well, I hope they never encounter it. That would be my prayer. It was enough to frighten someone to death, and to this day I still sleep upstairs in this old house. When I go to bed at night my bed is positioned to where I can always look out and see the night sky. Does that tell you anything after all these years?

> Mrs. Dolly Grady of 30th Street, said she had watched a similar UFO on Tuesday night for nearly an hour and said it had different colored lights.
>
> We watched it for about 10 minutes.

```
Case Number: WV-35559-105M
WITNESS NAME: DOLLY GRADY

Sighting Report: UFOs -- 30th Street
Description: Silver Object with 3 Lights
Report Date: November 1966
```

UFOs Over 30th Street

Amidst the heavy UFO and Men in Black encounters there seemed to be one area in upper Point Pleasant where many weird things were happening. The street where I lived was called 30th Street and intersected with nearby Jackson Avenue. 30th Street almost hosted a wide array of Mothman and UFO related witness including the home of Parke and Mabel McDaniel (parents of Linda Scarberry) where John Keel stayed and conducted many of his Mothman and UFO investigations. Living next door to the McDaniels was Dolly Grady and her family. After leaving church one evening in the nearby Bellemeade subdivision Dolly stared directly at a strange looking spacecraft hovering in the field across Jackson Avenue and then watched the object fly in the direction of 30th Street. Little did Dolly realize that she would be thrust into the middle of John Keel's quest for answers about the strange lights being seen in the skies of Point Pleasant.

In November of 1966 you lived five houses down from my family on 30th Street here in Point Pleasant. What were your thoughts at that time about the Mothman and UFO activity going on here?

Are you asking if I believe it happened?

Yes, I am.

Yes, I have a tendency to believe because their stories all basically stayed the same, and I do not believe that John Keel and some of the others who investigated what was happening, would have wasted their time here for as long as they did. He spent a lot of time in Point Pleasant. I don't think he would have stayed here if he had not felt that there was some substance to the story. I knew Parke and Mabel McDaniel (Linda Scarberry's parents) and their kids and I believe they saw something horrendous. I just believe they did.

Did you spend much time next door talking to the McDaniels and Linda?

Oh yes. I spent a lot of time at their house. Their kids and my kids all knew each other. I just don't think that they just thought something like that up.

Did you talk with John Keel during his stay next door with the McDaniel family?

I mostly listened. I didn't want to just barge in. They would invite me over and I would sit in and listen to their discussions. It was very interesting to me.

What do you recall about the November 15th sighting as reported by Linda Scarberry and the other three witnesses?

> **Mystery Bird Seen Flying Over Avenue**
>
> POINT PLEASANT — It looked like a bird as big as a plane and had legs like a man, the latest Mason Monster sighter reported.
>
> Mrs. Mabel McDaniel of 30th Street, Point Pleasant, said she saw a dark-colored flying creature with an extremely wide wingspan as she was driving on Jackson Avenue at about 5 p.m. Wednesday.
>
> Mrs. McDaniel is the mother of Mrs. Roger Scarberry, one of the original sighters of the bird-like creature popularly known as the "Mason Monster."
>
> A number of hunters have reported seeing owls, larger than normal size, in the Mason County area.

I do remember that Gary Northup, who at that time owned and operated Tiny's Drive-In at the end of 30th Street and who also lived beside of us, said that he didn't know what they had seen, but that he knew that he knew that those kids had seen something terrifying. (Note: Linda Scarberry stated that she and the other three witnesses ran into Tiny's and told Gary Northup what they has saw and asked him to notify the police on the evening of November 15th, 1966.)

I talked to a man who claims he was eating at Tiny's on the evening that Linda and the others ran into the restaurant to talk to Gary Northup. He said he had no doubt in his mind that they had been traumatized by something up in TNT. He said they were really shaken by the whole ordeal.

Gary told us that they were visibly shaken over what they had encountered.

> Page 2 — THE MESSENGER, Athens, Ohio — Friday, June 30, 1967
>
> **4 Boys Puzzled By Light In Sky**

During this time you witnessed some UFO activity in and around 30th Street?

I saw a lot of unidentified flying objects that I didn't feel were airplanes or anything of that sort. In John Keel's book, *The Mothman Prophecies*, he talks about how he and Mary Hyre, Mabel McDaniel, and others that would drive out to Five Mile road here in Point Pleasant. They would drive out this dirt road to a dead end where an old farmhouse was located. This is the exact location where my husband and I cut hay for our farm just in the past five years or so. I had forgotten over the years that what John Keel was writing about was basically our front door.

What did you witness just a few streets over from 30th Street on Bellemead Avenue during the Mothman and UFO sightings?

It was during John Keel's stay here, because he was at the McDaniel's home. It was early evening time and just beginning to get dark outside. I had gone to church at Bellemeade church that evening, which would have been a Wednesday night. It must have been around 8:30 or 9:00 pm. I had just pulled up to the main road after leaving the church, and there it was, just as big as anything. It was just hovering, not really moving, above the vacant field just on the other side of Jackson Avenue. I remember flooring the gas pedal as soon as I could get out onto Jackson Avenue, and when I did, this object took off at the same time. By the time I got over to 30th Street, I could see this object coming across the skyline. There were a lot of neighbors along with John Keel out there who saw it. It was moving in an upward direction directly over the vacant lot between our house and the McDaniel's house.

More UFOs Reported

POINT PLEASANT — More UFO sightings were reported Friday in the area of Point Pleasant. A woman said she looked out her window at 4 a.m. and saw a bright orange light hovering over houses on Jackson Avenue near Tiny's Drive-Inn.

Other people reported seeing lights around midnight also in the Point Pleasant area.

Many sightings have been reported by people residing in the Hartford and New Haven area in recent days.

Did the object make any type of noise or audible sounds? Where there any noticeable lights or other features?

No. It was just moving at a very fast rate of speed. There were three distinct colors of lights on the sides. There was a bright white light, a pastel-looking amber light, and an aqua-colored blue-green light.

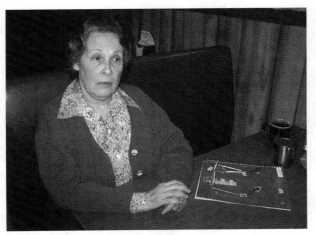

Do you feel that the UFOs and the Mothman sightings were somehow related?

All I know is that these things were all going on at the same time. I did not disbelieve any of the things that were happening.

Illustration by Gary Gibeaut

```
Case Number: WV-35559-106M
WITNESS NAME: DOTTIE CAMPBELL

Sighting Report: UFOs -- Jackson Avenue
Description: Cigar-Shaped Flying Object
Report Date: Fall 1966
```

They Were Dressed in Black

During 1966 Dottie Campbell and her family lived on Jackson Avenue near Tiny's drive-in on 30th Street and directly next door to local newspaper reporter Mary Hyre. Dottie would frequently visit with her close friend Mary by the fence in her backyard and listen with interest as Mary told her the newest details about all of the latest Mothman and UFO reports. By now a small group of witnesses and investigators were meeting regularly with people such as John Keel and Mary Hyre, the people spearheading the hunt for clues and explanations, and Dottie Campbell was one of those persons. In my interview with Dottie she speaks about Mary Hyre, the strange Men in Black that came to visit Mary, and some of the strange objects flying over Jackson Avenue.

Can you describe to me the overall mood or atmosphere here in Point Pleasant during 1966 and 1967 when the Mothman and UFO sightings were occurring?

I learned what was happening from Mary Hyre, who was my next door neighbor at that time. She worked long hours and very late, but then there were some days, like on a Saturday or Sunday, when she would be out in her backyard and we talked about things. She was more scared of the Men in Black than anything else. She told me that these men were parking across the street from her house in an older model black car and were visiting her frequently in her office in downtown Point Pleasant. They would show up dressed totally in black, and she said they never blinked their eyes. She felt like they were aliens trying to look like normal people and that's what frightened her so much. She told me they had an olive complexion. Mary talked often about John Keel and how they were both investigating some of the sightings and weird activities going on here in Point Pleasant.

So Mary Hyre was a writer for the local newspaper?

She wrote a column in the *Athens Messenger*. The newspaper had an office located downtown across from the courthouse on Sixth Street. Her column was called "Where the Waters Mingle."

So the Mothman story actually broke in the Athens Messenger *before the* Point Pleasant Register *newspaper ran it?*

Yes, it did.

When all of the Mothman sightings started to occur, was Mary Hyre at the forefront of the reporting?

Yes, there were a lot of sightings before anything else. That is when John Keel came here. Mary and John Keel would go down to Gallipolis Ferry and watch the UFO activity from a hill. A lot of people did that.

Do you believe that the Mothman sightings were somehow related to all of the UFO sightings in any way?

Mary Hyre was one of the top reporters for the Athens Messenger, *which had an office on 6th Street in Point Pleasant.*

Yes, I did. They seemed to be. We were having a big cookout one evening at our house on Jackson Avenue. We were having the cookout, and this UFO went over the house. It was like you could reach up and touch it. It was a cigar-shaped type object. It had lights on it and it moved over the house very slowly. You couldn't hear a thing. No sound whatsoever. It was so eerie. The kids called the police. They came up and asked everyone what they had been drinking. They acted like we were all crazy. Many people who saw things were afraid to report them out of fear of being made fun of or ridiculed.

Mary Hyre felt that the Mothman and UFO sightings were related somehow?

Yes, and she felt that these Men in Black were wanting to keep her quiet about it, so that she wouldn't be writing about these things in her columns. This is what really frightened her.

THE MESSENGER, Athens, Ohio — Monday, June 5, 1967 — Page 7

Sightings Reported In Point, New Haven

Did Mary ever discuss with you any of the conversations she had with these Men in Black? What type of questions were they asking her?

They asked her what she was writing about, and what business did she have writing about the sightings, and so forth. It was enough that they visited her quite often, and it scared her. Besides sitting in their cars in front of her house, she told me they would also sit in front of her office, too.

Did Mary ever say anything to you about her telephone lines being tapped or anything of that nature?

Yes, she did. She told me she would hear all sorts of noises on her phoneline. She thought it was all related to someone trying to listen in on her conversations concerning the sightings.

What are your thoughts on the Sandhill crane theory: do you think the Mothman sightings were really just someone seeing a large bird up in the TNT area?

No. I don't think it was that. I never believed that theory.

Mary Hyre was one of the first reporters to break the Mothman story. She and others would join John Keel in his investigation.

Monster Returns To Mason
By MARY HYRE

Winged, Red-Eyed 'Thing' Chases Point Couples Across Countryside

By MARY HYRE

EDITOR'S NOTE: Mary Hyre, Point Pleasant correspondent for The Messenger, has written many stories in the past eight months about UFO sightings in the Mason County area. Last week she attended a UFO watchers' convention in New York City. In this story, she describes her experiences.)

By MARY HYRE
Point Pleasant Correspondent

Last Saturday night I was invited by John A. Keel, a well-known writer, to appear with him on the Long John Nebel radio show on NBC which has an endless parade of saucer personalities.

A strange woman also appeared on the show who claimed she was Miss Venus from the planet Venus.

Others on this show who questioned Miss Venus for over four hours were sports broadcaster Mel Allen, the popular radio and TV personality Art Ford and writers of New York papers. While none believed her story, it did leave everyone baffled just who she was and where she came from. She also appeared at the UFO convention the next day. This is the story she told and some of the questions she was asked.

Miss Venus claimed she came to Earth on Sept. 27, seven years ago as double for a girl who committed suicide on that date and has lived with the girl's parents, who are not aware that she is not their daughter. She has worked at various jobs using the other girl's name and Social Security number, which she would not

Where The Waters Mingle
By MARY HYRE

What does a strange monster do to a town or a community? Or one might ask what happens at the news desk of a paper! Since the strange creature was sighted in this area this week it has brought more excitement than anything I have witnessed since I started working for The Messenger nearly 25 years ago.

I always said nothing could compare with a flood back in the days when the town would be covered just about every year, but this has created more turmoil and fear for many.

I don't care where you go, you can hear it being asked: "Wonder what the latest is on the thing that has been hovering over the area?"

While some are curious about it, others are afraid to leave their homes at night. People who have been to other cities this week say that is all you can hear.

One lady said, "This could only happen in Mason County," I think it is a good county and maybe the monster picked a good one to come to, what ever it might be, a creature or a man from another planet.

My phone rings constantly about this happening and if I could print all of it I would have to write a book. Some have some cute sayings while others are very serious and concerned.

"It is the Gallipolis Blue Devil football team, coming over to haunt the Big Blacks," said one, while another said, "It's only the Democrats coming back from Salt Creek with red eyes."

Rumors Friday flooded the office saying, "Why did they kill the eagle, why didn't they catch and put it on display so that people could see it."

The Steve Mallette and Roger Scarberry families who first saw this creature don't appreciate all the jokes that are being said, and I don't blame them.

The wife of a prominent businessman a few weeks ago during the day saw an object flying. She said it wasn't an airplane, but resembled a butterfly, between 10 and 15 feet long. She said she was afraid to tell anyone fearing they might laugh at her.

The traffic continued to grow Friday night when a constant stream of cars, flowed into the TNT area.

Ed Brown, director) of the West Virginia Security Service, a private detective concern, is interested in contacting any person who may have seen the monster. He would like to talk with the people, whose names will never be revealed, for research and evaluation. He may be reached by sending mail to Ed Brown, Charleston or phone 925-9851.

ARCHIVES:
UFOs and Men in Black

RECENT NEWS

"MYSTERY MAN" NABBED ON LONG ISLAND: (Special to SAUCER NEWS from John Keel.) Those elusive "Men in Black" were reportedly busy again throughout the Country this summer, and at least two of them fell into unexpected traps in the New York area. One is supposed to have been killed in the streets of the city, while the other was suddenly taken into custody by unidentified legal authorities.

Several teams of men in black turtleneck sweaters visited eight separate communities in the state of Washington in April, allegedly warning UFO witnesses not to discuss what they had seen. They told some people that they represented Civil Defense and were trying to prevent a panic, but since most Civil Defense operations were disbanded two years ago, this seems unlikely.

Citizens in Canada, Maine, New Jersey, California, and Long Island, N.Y. also told of being visited by "government men" this spring. One of these witnesses says he was ordered to turn over some flying saucer pictures "for the sake of yourself, your family, and your world." (See story on Page 14.)

In West Virginia, Mr. Tad Jones, who witnessed a hovering sphere on a major highway on January 19th, received two threatening notes warning him not to tell anyone what he had seen. These notes were crudely printed on cheap paper and cardboard and slipped under his door in Dunbar, W. Va. One of the notes was somehow set afire after being shoved under the door, and the edges were badly burned.

The printing on these "prank" warnings was identical to the printing on a note placed under the door of a UFO sighter in Middleport, Ohio. This girl, who had allegedly seen West Virginia's famous "Moth Man", later escaped from a would-be kidnapper - a tanned young man who was driving an old car "that looked like new." Police in Middleport were baffled. There was no one in the area who resembled the girl's description of her assailant.

On Long Island, two men in Air Force uniforms harassed UFO witnesses. One of these men identified himself as "Lt. Frank Davis" and threatened two different people with a revolver, warning them to "watch out who you talk to." A "Colonel John Dalton" interviewed at least three Long Island residents and asked them to fill out complicated forms which contained involved questions about the witnesses' personal history. Through officials on Long Island, John Keel had a check run on both men. The Air Force denied that it knew anything about either one, or that men with those names were assigned anywhere on the Island.

"Lt. Davis" later turned up in a postman's uniform and was followed by Keel. "Davis" and another man were engaged in taking photographs of the homes of UFO sighters. While involved in this investigation, Keel had two encounters with a large black Cadillac in an isolated section of Long Island. In one of these encounters, the Cadillac, which contained two dark-skinned men, was parked and laying in wait on a deserted road. In the other incident, Keel did a turnabout and followed the Caddie for several miles.

On August 4th, a black Cadillac made a deliberate attempt to run over a UFO witness on the main street of a small Long Island town.

One of the "mystery men" known to be involved in the Long Island capers was reportedly killed in New York City by unknown assailants on July 28th. "Lt. Davis" was apprehended on August 5th by agents from an unidentified law agency. "Davis" was in a public place when two well-dressed men approached him and forcibly removed him. All three men then drove away in a large black car, either a Cadillac or a Lincoln, according to the many witnesses. "Colonel Dalton" is believed to be still at large.

Strange hoax calls continued throughout the summer, involving UFO researchers in many states. Some Ufologists received as many as three or four calls daily, and at all hours. The hoaxters were able, somehow, to get unlisted phone numbers. None of the calls could be traced. These calls were received in West Virginia; Connecticut; Washington, D.C; Massachusetts; Ontario, Canada; Long Island, N.Y; and many other places. Some were threats delivered in accented voices. Others consisted only of eerie electronic sounds.

All in all, it was a hectic summer, and quite possibly only a taste of even stranger events yet to come.

"I see a man in a dark suit coming into your life"

"MAN IN BLACK" CASE IN OHIO: Following a pattern which has become fairly commonplace during the past few months, weird events began happening to Robert Easley soon after he returned to his home in Defiance, Ohio, after attending the UFO Convention in New York City. Easley, incidentally, is a respected saucer researcher, holding positions of importance in several UFO organizations, including that of Ohio Director of the Interplanetary News Service.

In the wee hours of July 11th, Mr. Easley was awakened by a phone call from a lady who told him that she and seven others were observing two bright, fast-moving UFOs. After she hung up, he immediately got dressed and went to the scene. While checking out this report, he noticed that he was being followed by a man in a black sedan with no license plates. The driver - a complete stranger to Easley - was dressed in black shoes, black dress pants, and a dark blue pullover shirt.

On July 15th, he was again followed by the same man in the same car as he was driving his girl friend home. When he pulled into her driveway the unknown car sped off. Later that evening, as the two sat talking on the front porch, the car came down the road and stopped right in front of the house, as soon as the topic of UFOs entered the conversation. Easley could feel the man staring at them. When they got off the subject of UFOs the car left, but when they got back on it about an hour later, the same car came back again. It was as if the mysterious driver could hear what they were saying or read their minds!

On July 17th, as Mr. Easley was checking out another rather routine UFO report, the man reappeared and followed him to and from the scene of the sighting, dressed in apparently the same clothes as before.

FALL, 1967
Price: 50 cents

SAUCER NEWS

OFFICIAL PUBLICATION OF THE SAUCER AND UNEXPLAINED CELESTIAL EVENTS RESEARCH SOCIETY

Mailing Address:
P.O. BOX 163,
FORT LEE, N.J. 07024

Editor:
James W. Moseley
Managing Editor:
Michael Cleveland

Office:
303 FIFTH AVE., Suite 816
NEW YORK, N.Y. 10016
Telephone: 212-686-3743

Volume 14, Number 3
Whole Number **69**

← SHOWN HERE, left to right, are writer John Keel, publisher Gray Barker, and Chairman James Moseley, during an intermission between public sessions of the 1967 Congress of Scientific Ufologists in New York. (Photo courtesy of George Earley.)

See centerfold of this issue for more pictures of the Convention.

CONTENTS OF THIS ISSUE

Editorial..Page 3
Editorial Notes...Page 5
Recent News..Page 11
Letters to the Editor...Page 23
Book Reviews - by Timothy Green Beckley..........................Page 28
Recent UFO Sightings..Page 32

FEATURE ARTICLES:

The UFO Secret: Answers Are on the Way - by John A. Keel............Page 6
The Nature of the UFO and NICAP - by Steve Erdmann...................Page 8

Preceding pages: John Keel's own investigative report detailing Men in Black encounters. The article was featured in Saucer Smear *magazine. (Courtesy of James Moseley and Saucer Smear)*

One who claims to have talked with the occupant of a UFO is Woodrow Derenberger of Mineral Wells, W. Va., a small community near Parkersburg.

Mr. Derenberger's strange experience was on Nov. 2, 1966, about 7 p. m. while he was driving toward Parkersburg on Interstate 77 from Marietta, O. He is a salesman working in the Parkersburg area.

An object came into view alongside his panel truck and was traveling at about the same speed. The object settled to the highway in front of him causing him to stop.

Mr. Derenberger described the craft as dark or charcoal grey, with a metallic appearance and shaped like an old kerosene lamp globe turned on its side. The thing had a flat bottom and a dome light near the top.

A door swung open and out stepped a man with very "human-like features." The old-looking man approached his car and told him to roll down the window.

The visitor was said to have been wearing "a short topcoat with trousers that could be seen beneath the coat and a shirt buttoned at the neck." The clothes, Mr. Derenberger said, were blue and quite shiny, having a glistening effect."

Although Mr. Derenberger said he communicated with the strange being for five or 10 minutes, the visitor did not move his lips. Mr. Derenberger said the mans communication was by "thought waves or mental telepathy." He said the visitor smiled constantly.

The man from the craft was described as being six feet tall, 35 to 40 years old, 185 pounds, and having a dark complexion. Mr. Derenberger was asked by the man what the lights were in the distance and he told the visitor that the lights were from the city of Parkersburg.

"What is a Parkersburg," the man asked. Mr. Derenberger explained that it was a place where people lived. The man then said that such a place where he was from would be called a "gathering."

The most baffling part of the salesman's experience was that the stranger told him "Have no fear, we come from a country that is not nearly as powerful as yours. We mean you no harm."

Mr. Derenberger said after the visitor finished talking the saucer took off at tremendous speed.

Shortly after reaching his home Mr. Derenberger telephoned Parkersburg police.

As is common after such a report is made public, the press gave wide coverage to the story and shortly afterward, Mr. Derenberger had his telephone number unlisted, presumably because of pranksters and hecklers.

Mr. Derenberger is known as a respected man in his community, the father of two small children and attends church regularly.

A reported sighting of a UFO was also made Jan. 18,

There have been many sightings of the "Moth Man" all up and down the Ohio Valley since I left West Virgina. And there was a UFO landing reported on a highway outside Charleston, a few miles south of Point Pleasant, on January 19th, 1967." Early in January, Mrs. Mary Hyre, the Point Pleasant correspondent for the Athens (Ohio) *Messenger*, and a newspaper-woman of some 25 years experience, received a strange visitor in her office. (Mrs. Hyre accompanied me during many of my investigations in the area and she wrote a number of stories about the UFO sightings. Since she is an AP stringer, many of her stories go out on the wire across the country.) She was working late in her office across from the County Court House when a little man entered. He was about 4' 6" tall, she told me recently on the telephone, and had very strange eyes covered with thick-lensed glasses. His black hair was long and cut squarely "like a bowl haircut". Although it was about 20°F outside, he was wearing a short-sleeved blue shirt and blue trousers. He kept his right hand in his pocket at all times.

Speaking in a slow, halting voice, he asked her for directions to Welsh, West Virgina. She thought at first that he had some kind of speech impediment, and for some reason he terrified her. "He kept getting closer." Alarmed, she ran into the back room where the newspaper's circulation manager was working on a telephone campaign. He joined her and they spoke together to the little man. "He seemed to know more about West Virginia than we did," she declared. At one point the telephone rang and while she was speaking on it the little man picked up a ballpoint pen from her desk and looked at it in amazement, "as if he had never seen a pen before". She gave him a pen and said he laughed in a loud, strange way as he took it. Then he ran out into the night and disappeared around a corner.

Being a good newspaper-woman, Mrs. Hyre later checked with the police to find out if there was any mentally deficient person on the loose who fitted the little man's description. There wasn't."

Opposite: *A rare manuscript page compiled by John Keel detailing the Mothman story prior to publication of* The Mothman Prophecies.

UFO Rumors Flying

BY JEAN WARNER

Rumors of Unidentified Flying Objects were rampant Wednesday night in the Meigs-Mason-Gallia County areas while residents even plaguing police phones with reports of various sightings.

Many took to the outdoors scanning the sky and confirmed reports than an illuminous object, not like any seen before, was sighted flying in many directions and from high and low altitudes.

Charlie Wood, Emergency Officer at the Point Pleasant Station, reports some kind of disruption with police radios for a period shortly after dark, but later this cleared.

Several persons, including two Mason County residents, have reported seeing or hearing unidentified flying objects over this county, on Monday and Tuesday nights.

A Point Pleasant woman, who asked not to be identified, reports of hearing an unusual sound hovering around her home on the northern outskirts of town early Tuesday morning.

She said she had gone to bed, but was not asleep around 1:30 a.m. when she heard the noise "an unusual one which sounded like it was whipping around in a circle". She said "It would go for a distance, would get closer and louder and then went away again."

Thinking it sounded like what she had heard before on television, to be a space ship, she felt it too iroical to be true, but never-the-less felt apprehensive. Looking out the windows, she was unable to see anything and described herself as "too scared" to actually go outside. She reports hearing the noise off and on for a two hour period.

Last night, a Crab Creek resident told of seeing flashing from two red lights about 8:30 p.m. She said those seen were while she was standing in her yard, when one object seemed to come up river and the other from the Lower Five Mile area on a hill. She tells they appeared to meet while revolving around, flashing red, and then changing to a solid blueish-green color. She heard no sound, but said they apeared to be very low and were not like anything she had seen before.

Several reports of UFO sightings have been made in West Virginia and Ohio within the past few days.

Several persons, including a weather observer and a pilot experienced in night flying, reported seeing an unidentified flying object over the Raleigh County Airport Monday night.

The object first appeared about 8:45 p.m. and remained for about 30 to 40 minutes, according to Howard Moneypenny, weather service specialist for the National Oceanic and Atmosphere Administration.

"It had no definitive shape and I have no idea how far away or how big it was," he said. "Our visibility was unlimited at the time and there was just no way of telling."

The airport does not have radar, but virtually all employes reported seeing the object. It was described as having red, green and white flashing lights.

The pilot, who asked not be identified, said he took off in a Cessna 182 to pursue the object, which moved away from him toward the Bolt Mountain area.

"It just kept moving away from me. I couldn't get any closer," he said. "I don't think it was an airplane because the whole thing would change color at the same time."

It was the first UFO sighting in West Virginia, although numerous sightings have been occurring across the nation in recent weeks.

►Woodrow Derenberger, formerly of Parkersburg, said that on the night of Nov. 2, 1966, a "dark hulk" descended in front of his van truck on I-77 near Parkersburg and forced him to stop. As the gray metallic object hovered over the pavement, he said, a man emerged from a door in it, walked to Derenberger's car and "talked" to him by extrasensory perception. The stranger said his name was "Cold" and that he came from "a country much less powerful than yours," Derenberger claimed. After the wordless chat, the visitor re-entered his craft and rose into the sky, he said.

►Another unidentified flying object listed in Barker's West Virginia tabulation is "mothman," a mysterious bird reported in various parts of the state for several years.

He says a Point Pleasant woman told him she first saw the creature on W.Va. 2 in 1961, describing it as man-sized and with "a set of huge wings that filled the entire width of the road." Also, she said, a bird-like thing "bumped" on the roof of her house and emitted "high-pitched beeping sounds" somewhat like electronic noises.

►The weirdest report in Barker's

Unusual Objects In Sky Spotted In Three Counties

POINT PLEASANT —UFO's have made quite a display since Sunday night in three counties, Mason, Putnam and Roane.

Sunday night just before dark a long, black object with no wings or any visable gear glided very low over Point Pleasant.

A few hours later north of Point Pleasant, several people saw a white light very low in the east. Among the people seeing the bright light was John A. Keel, a noted Ufologist, writer and lecturer. Keel has done extensive research on UFO sightings and has traveled many miles during the past year.

The white light was visable for about ten minutes, bobbed up and down and suddenly vanished.

A Putnam County man, Albert Brown, a shift superintendent at the new mining operations at Elmwood, reported that when he left work at 12:45 Monday morning he noticed a strange white light very low as he traveled toward his Buffalo home. On Tribble Road and Route 35, this oject stayed in his view.

He said he finally stopped and watched the UFO, and it turned colors of blue and orange and bobbed up and down. It would first be on top of the hill, then disappear behind the hill and then reappear. He tried to find a road that would lead him to where it seemed to be stationary, but was unable to do so.

He noted that he parked his truck and watched the object for about four hours and then went home and awakened his wife, Shirley, to show her what he had seen. She reported that it was the brightest and strangest light she had ever seen.

Brown, deciding that this was something that should be investigated, called the Civil Defense in Charleston. But they told him to call the state police.

The object had gone by the time they arrived.

Mrs. Brown said she had received a call from Gary Davison, Spencer, who said he had seen a similar object in the Spencer area Sunday evening about 7 p.m.

(ADVERTISEMENT)

HAS YOUR DRUGGIST RECOMMENDED THIS COLD REMEDY?

If he hasn't, he may do so. For the reason it is dependable and effective and most druggists insist on this . . . yet is 100% free of narcotics ingredients. Contains only time-tested ingredients.

Reliable Casco Cold Tablets do not cause unexpected side effects. Do not upset your nervous system, nor do they cause drastic allergic reaction that your druggist may say is wrong for you.

Yet . . . Casco Cold Tablets work within minutes to give you the relief you want. "Best cold remedy the world has ever known." "Have always helped." Comments like these are typical.

That's why Casco Cold Tablets are guaranteed — even in cases of chronic colds — to give prompt relief or money back from the maker.

Meetings In Meigs

Illustration by Gary Gibeaut

It Was a Bird...a Huge Bird

Just days after the first Mothman sightings at the North Power Plant, Tom Ury of Point Pleasant was up early to make a trip back to Clarksburg, WV. Tom was the manager of a shoe store there, and needed to head back in time for the Thanksgiving holiday shopping rush that was about to begin. At about 8am, just outside of Point Pleasant, Tom would find himself peering out of his windshield staring at a giant, dark bird circling above his car.

I have known Tom for a number of years. I remember reading about his encounter in Mr. Keel's book, and the original press clippings compiled by reporter Mary Hyre that appeared first in the *Athens Messenger* and then the *Point Pleasant Register* when the event took place on the early morning hours of November 25th, 1966. From the very beginning, Tom was adamant that what he saw that early November morning was a very large bird that began to circle his car, getting closer with each rotation. With numerous Mothman or "big bird" sightings that same week, Tom immediately contacted the sheriff in Mason County and told him what had happened. He would discover that he was not the first person to file a report with the Sheriff's office.

Tom always told me he wanted a forum to explain the details of that day, because he felt some of his story had gotten mixed around or had been left out in the past. One of the unique aspects of Tom's ordeal is that he was the first witness to see this thing in broad daylight, and would be able to give fairly accurate estimates as to how big it was, and at what speeds it could fly. The following detailed account is of that early morning drive to work that Tom finds hard to forget.

You are mentioned in Gary Barker's book The Silver Bridge. Did you know Mr. Barker and had you ever spoke to him about your experience?

You know I never realized that Barker's office was right upstairs from the shoe store where I used to work in Clarksburg, West Virginia. I had just returned back to town from Hutchinson, Kansas, and was in there talking to the old manager of the store. The subject of Mothman came up and I said, "Man, I would like to meet that Gray Barker about the stuff he wrote in his book." It was years later, after 1966, before I had ever read his book. A friend of mine named "Fuzzy" Farley had a copy of it and I read what he had wrote in there. Just about that time Mr. Barker walked in the door. Bernie, the manager, said, "Well, there comes Gray Barker now." Bernie introduced us, and I told Mr. Barker that I wanted to speak to him. We had a good chat there, and then he walked back upstairs and that is when he autographed the book for me. But he was straightforward about what he called "poetic license." He said that's the way we wrote in this type business of science fiction, etc., etc. He would tell you that he wrote the book in a fairy-tale style.

So you never really sat down and talked to Mr. Barker, prior to his release of the book in the early 1970s?

No. I never had an interview with anybody until just about three years ago. Because I was in the newspaper articles from that first week of sightings, my story was used in the later books on the Mothman. I had never met Mr. Barker or Mr. Keel and had never been interviewed by either author. I reported my story to Mary Hyre who then featured it in the local newspapers. It was fairly accurate from what I told Mary.

Did you know Mary Hyre very well?

I used to deliver the *Athens Messenger* in addition to the *Point Pleasant Register*. About a month after that article came out, I came back down to Point Pleasant, and I walked down to her office on main street. I said, "Mary, I ought to shoot you," jokingly. I told her the article was close to the mark, except that article claimed that the huge bird rose up from the trees on the right side of the road. It came from the left where the river bank (Ohio River) is and it went back to the river bank. I felt she made it seem that the bird came from the direction of the TNT area. She told me not to worry too much about it, because in a month or two this whole Mothman flap would all pass over (insert laughter). Here we are 40 years after it happened and people are still talking about it.

When I first saw this giant bird, I never stated that I watched it take off straight up in the air from the side of the road like a helicopter. The two couples who saw this thing in TNT described it as doing that. The only time I had ever mentioned a helicopter was to Mary Hyre, and I told her that when I first saw it out of the corner of my eye (which would have been about a 1/4 of a mile from Route 62 over to the river bank). It reminded me of something out of an Arnold Swartzenegger or Sylvester Stallone movie where the silent helicopter rises up over the treetops. That is what it looked like when I first saw it.

How big would you say the wingspan was?

Oh, my goodness. When I first spotted it, I really thought it was a helicopter, because I could not hear any noise at all, but it was not really that close to my car yet. But then it rose over the trees, and proceeded to make the big circles just like a normal bird would fly. It started out at approximately 500 feet up in the air, but each time it would make a circle I could see it every time it came in front of my car. I don't know what it did behind the car. It was coming lower and lower at this time. The last pass that it made was probably only 75 feet over the top of my car.

At that time I had a pretty good shot at it, and the only thing that I could try to judge it by, was the

> POINT PLEASANT — Mason County's famous "bird" is apparently still with us and has made its appearance in the daytime for the first time.
>
> Tom Ury, a Clarksburg resident, told the sheriff's office he had an experience with the "bird"" this morning at 7:15 a.m., as he traveled north on Route 62.
>
> Ury, an assistant manager of the Kinney Store at Clarksburg, was enroute back to the northern city after spending Thanksgiving here with relatives when he encountered the "bird."
>
> "I know people think you're crazy when you tell of seeing something like this," Ury said, "but I've never had such an experience. I was scared."
>
> In giving an account to the Register, the frightened young man said as he went up the road he spotted a flying object that seemed to come from the woods on his right.
>
> After his description of the area, it was determined it came from the area back of the Homer Smith residence.
>
> "It came up like a helicopter and then veered over my car. It began going around in circles about two or three telephone poles high and kept staying over my car," he added.
>
> While his first thought was that of fear, Ury noted, "I tried to get away and was going 70 miles an hour, but it kept up with me easily."
>
> He stated that it kept soaring over his vehicle until he got to the Kirkland Memorial Gardens and then it made its way to the left and over the river.
>
> Apparently still shook up, Ury said, "I have a convertible and at first felt it was going to come through the top, but after it stayed in the air at about the same height, I didn't feel it would attack."

Tom Ury's encounter with a large bird while driving his car makes headlines in newspapers across the region the following day.

fact that I used to play a lot of basketball in high school and I knew the foul line to the basket was 15 feet. I would guess the wingspan was at least 10 to 12 feet wide with both wings extended. I have seen quite a few hawks from when I lived in Clarksburg, which was mountain terrain. This thing was nothing like that.

It wasn't a Sandhill Crane. I don't care what Professor Smith (West Virginia University) said. Here is a man who never came to Point Pleasant, and basically took newspaper accounts to draw his conclusion that this thing people were seeing was nothing more than a crane. He could have called me or Everett Wedge (Mr. Wedge spotted the large bird at the nearby Gallipolis, Ohio airport in November, 1966) who thought it was an airplane because of its massive size. Nobody ever called.

But this thing was an abnormally sized bird....

Oh, my goodness. I would not have reported it if I thought it was just an eagle or a hawk even with that big of a wingspan. It was only later on that I read about the maximum wingspan on a bird.

Did it have fairly quick speed?

It made about four passes, and I was just past the Kirkland Memorial Cemetery on the right side of the highway. Then, there is the real long straight stretch of road, and I had a great big Ford Fairlane 500 with an Interceptor V8 engine and that thing would mosey. I told George Johnson (Mason County sheriff) that I was going 75 miles per hour when I hit the straight stretch. I remember jokingly asking him not to issue me a speeding ticket. Towards the end of the long section of road, I was doing about 90 miles per hour. I then

started to slow the car down after the bird went back over towards the river. It came from the river and went back towards the river. I don't know if it was nesting over there or what.

What time of the morning did all of this happen?

Well, I had left early to get to Clarksburg, where I managed the shoe store. This was November 25th and we were getting ready for one of our busiest days of the year at the store. The assistant manager told me he would open the store, since I had returned to Point Pleasant to visit with my family for the Thanksgiving holiday. I told him that I would come in at 1pm, and keep the store open until 9pm. I started up Route 62 at around 7:45am. People have asked me why I took Route 62 to drive to Clarksburg, instead of the normal Route 2 to Ravenswood, West Virginia. At that time, they were widening Route 50 into a four lane highway, like it is today, so I would drive up on the Ohio side to save some travel time.

Were there any other cars in front or behind you when this happened?

I really can't say for sure. I do not ever remember seeing a car on the way up. I drove on to Mason, West Virginia, to a little gas station at the foot of the Mason bridge, where I called Sheriff Johnson in Point Pleasant. That was the only time that I had ever told anyone semi-jokingly that I think I had seen their "Mothman." From that time on, I always told people that I has seen a large bird. Sheriff Johnson asked me if I would drive back down to Point Pleasant, and that he would send a deputy up to investigate things. I told him that this bird was big enough to eat me and the deputy both. I told him that I was okay, and that the bird had went back over towards the river. I drove back down to his office in the courthouse.

When I arrived Mary Hyre was already there in his office. Apparently, in the time it took me to drive back from Mason, back down to the courthouse, word must have gotten out

Large bird reported flying over area Tuesday evening

There is a growing number of witnesses testifying to seeing abnormally large birds, possibly beyond anything known to the ordinary ornithologist.

Several such sightings of a "large, black bird" have been reported recently by the United Press International in Indiana and Illinois.

In the 1960s there was the "Mason County Monster" that frightened at least two groups of people at night driving along Route 62 in their cars. Neither sighting ever was satisfactorily explained. The monster — with reddish fiery eyes — was reported as far away as Louisiana later.

James Schoolcraft, of 25 Smithers St., Gallipolis, perhaps was made a believer of the big bird stories Tuesday evening. "People may laugh at me (they already had, he hinted) but I saw it. There was no doubt about what I saw," he said today.

Schoolcraft said he was at a softball game on the Elks field and left it momentarily on a personal errand. Upon leaving the nearby Price field, looking up, Schoolcraft observed at an elevation he guessed to be 800 to 900 feet a huge bird with a wingspan appearing to be 10 to 12 feet, black, with a long, curving neck, flying west. He said much smaller birds seemed to be chasing it, attempting to mount an attack but the monster bird gave them no heed.

Asked the elevation of what he saw, Schoolcraft gave the figures above, but admitted he had no practice in guessing elevation accurately. "It was high enough to fly over the surrounding hills with good clearance," he said.

And he offered this final bit of sobering testimony: "I don't drink."

---

about what I had seen. Mary's office was just directly across the street from the courthouse. The sheriff was very interested in what I had to say, and he knew that I was a reputable person.

Were you a little bit shaken at this time?

Yeah, I guess I was scared to a certain extent. But then, when I realized that this thing was not going to attack me or anything, I did not feel as threatened. When it first started getting lower, it seemed to be more curious about me...almost a mutual curiosity. After that, it wasn't that I was scared, but I was apprehensive. I have to say that I was relieved when it went back towards the river. But it got my curiosity, and I remember saying to myself, What in the world? I've never seen anything that big!

I have tried to rethink and rehash the whole thing, but to me it was a bird, and of course, after nearly 40 years, there are some details that I don't remember. I do not remember ever seeing it flap its wings, but when you are driving like I was, looking through the top of your windshield, I could only see it making the big circles, almost like a predatory bird. It may have been flapping its wings when I could not see it, and then only gliding when it came around the front where I could get a clear view of it. That is another reason why I could never describe a head or feet because it was always flying away from me, but I could tell the body was pretty good size.

Some of the witnesses have described to me that the body looked almost like that of a man with legs.

Legs I could not see, because I think that most birds, when in flight, have their legs folded up underneath them. The body to me was large, but I wouldn't say it was as large as a man, but it was big enough to support the wingspan that it had. It wasn't a little skinny two-pound body supporting fifty pounds of wings.

Did it have any feathers?

Yeah, it had feathers. It was a ruffled looking bird. It was not a sleek, shiny looking bird like a crow or anything. It was a brownish, grayish, blackish, ugly looking thing. I told one reporter that it looked to me like a "Mr. Bird that had just gotten out of bed with a Mrs. Bird," all ruffled up and everything. It was not a pretty bird.

You did not see any prominent red eyes?

Like I said, I could not make any type of a head or anything, but man, that thing could move. I was going 75 miles per hour, and it's making circles and still keeping up with me and getting lower each time.

When you arrived to speak to the sheriff, did he mention any of the other witnesses and their accounts, and had you already heard about some of those reports in the newspapers?

I had heard about it by talking to my mother on the phone when calling from Clarksburg. I didn't laugh it off, because I was curious, but reports of a man with wings? I don't refute anybody's story. I know what I saw, but who is to say somebody else saw something different? I have never seen a man with wings, and I don't intend to. I can't tell people who say they have seen a man with wings that they are making the story up. If that is what they claim to have seen, then I have no reason not to believe them. My personal opinion is that what these people were seeing was this large bird at night.

What action did the sheriff plan to take after all of these reports?

He said that they had received other reports, and that he would send a deputy up there to check things out, and see if they could spot anything. I told him that this thing never

landed in the vicinity that I was in. I told him that I would check in and see what had developed, and I tried to just keep things quiet, so to speak. By the time I arrived in Clarksburg, I don't know how in the world it had gotten out, but I was getting calls from Australia, Los Angeles, Detroit. Most of these calls were from radio talk shows, asking if I had seen this so-called "man with wings." I told them I had seen a huge bird. The story had probably been sent out over the wire through Mary Hyre. It was a little annoying for a few days, and I took some ribbing off of my friends. It died off after awhile, and when I would come back to Point Pleasant, most people knew that I was pretty level headed.

You mentioned to me that your mother had a few experiences possibly tied to your reporting of this large bird?

She didn't tell me for years about some of those things. She was a very straight-laced woman. She said she would hear strange noises on the telephone line when she would pick up the phone to make a call…some were similar to some of the things John Keel wrote about. She told me the phone would ring in the middle of the night and when she picked it up, she could only hear something that resembled morse code. Lights in the house would go out and everyone else's lights would still be on.

Did she think that these events were related to your sighting?

Yes, to a certain extent. She never had any Men in Black visit her. If they did, then they outsmarted me. If they were wearing a black suit, I would have probably thought they were a Pentecostal minister or something. There were a lot of things she never got around to telling before she passed away this year. She never really opened up about it until a year or so ago. I think she kept a lot of it to herself. She was never into being in the public eye.

Did you know any of the other witnesses at that time?

I did know Roger Scarberry from school, and he and my brother ran around together. They both had hot rods at that time. I never knew Roger to exaggerate on anything. It shocked me when all of the stories came out in the papers about them seeing the Mothman up in TNT. To me he didn't seem like the type to make up a story, and that is one reason why I have always held out that these people saw something.

If it had been some of the other people that age that I knew, I would have probably thought differently. He was just a common, ordinary guy and he was not looking for publicity or notoriety. He had come to our house on occasion, and he was a real quiet, laid-back boy and real mannerful. I think many people living here at that time felt that if someone spoke up or received any limelight, so to speak, then they were either drinking or on drugs. Here I am, going back to work, 150 miles from here to a respectable job. I had nothing to gain by even telling anyone what I saw, but I felt that it was newsworthy. I was never bothered by the ridicule because I still stand behind my original story.

What do you remember about Mary Hyre and how involved was she in the whole Mothman-UFO flap?

I liked Mary because she was always good to me. Mary was very good at reporting local news. I don't care if a woman was sewing a quilt, Mary could make a news story out of it and the people here liked local news. Mary Hyre and Jack Rodgers were probably the best local newspaper people because they knew what the local people wanted to read.

I am glad we could finally sit down and discuss your story. Thanks for confiding in me about what you saw that morning in 1966.

Thank you…I enjoyed talking to you about it.

Photographs of the actual owl that was shot and killed on the Ace Henry farm in Gallipolis Ferry, West Virginia, as detailed in the press clippings on the opposite page. Many thought the Mothman was actually a large owl or sandhill crane.

Giant Owl Killed On Area Farm

Bird Killed 12-22-66

A bird although a dead one, is in the news again and the big question is — Is it or isn't it one that may have been spotted here on several occasions?

Apparently from the discription it is not the one that was seen by two young couples last month, but may be one that has kept cropping into headlines since that time.

A large owl uncommon to this area, was killed Tuesday night by Ace Henry on his farm at Gallipolis Ferry.

The bird, which has a wing spread of nearly five feet, has several areas of white and is speckled with black. On the under side of the wings the plumage is snowy white, and white fur-like feathers encircle the large eyes and cover the claws.

Henry said he shot it with a 20-gauge shotgun Tuesday night after it was spotted sitting on top of his barn. He said at first he thought it was a hawk but after killing it he was perplexed to know its true identity.

The Register Editorial staff, in an attempt to identify the bird, has concluded that it is a snowy owl.

The snowy owl is an inhabitant of northern regions, where his coloring blends with the snowy surroundings. In the winter it travels south through the states and sometimes as far as Texas. On the wing it is so swift that it will overtake a grouse in flight.

Not Mason Mothman, Is It An Owl?

POINT PLEASANT — Point Pleasant may well be tagged "Birdland" if bird stories and bird sightings continue to make news locally.

The newest story concerns another large, strange bird. However, this one is dead.

Ace Henry of Gallipolis Ferry, saw a large bird perched on his barn Tuesday night, and thinking it was a hawk shot it with a 20-gauge shotgun.

Henry reports the bird has a wingspan of about five feet and is two feet tall. The underside of the wings are white, and the rest is speckled with gray, with white rough around its eyes and white feathers covering its claws.

He said the bird is identical to a picture he has of a snowy owl. The snowy owl breeds in the Artic and migrates as far south as the Caribbean Sea.

Illustration by Gary Gibeaut

```
Case Number: WV-35559-108M
WITNESS NAME: DARREN HAYES

Sighting Report: TNT Area--Fairgrounds Road
Description: Dark Winged Creature
Report Date: Early 1990s
```

The Chase is On

Not all Mothman encounters took place back in 1966-67. Reports flood in to my email address almost daily describing a giant, winged figure flying over their car or a giant bird-like creature virtually appearing out of nowhere. My interest has always been in the unexplainable encounters here and around the Point Pleasant area, past and present, so the interview I conducted with Darren Hayes suggests that not all is normal even today in the TNT area. Again it was obvious to me that while talking about his experience, Darren felt very uneasy and hesitant in describing what he saw that night in the early 1990s. Is the Mothman or "big bird" still roaming the desolate grounds of TNT area still today?

Do you remember the time frame that your sighting occurred?

Yes, it happened about 15 years ago. It was in the late 80s, or early 90s. It was around Christmas time. We had gone out looking at Christmas lights that evening.

Were you familiar with the TNT area at that time?

I was familiar with it, only from the fact that my aunt had taken me there when I was a little kid to the pond areas to fish. I had not been in the TNT area for years, so we just decided to drive back through there that night.

Can you tell me exactly what happened after you arrived in the TNT area?

Yes. Like I mentioned, we were driving around looking at Christmas lights in Mason, West Virginia, and we were headed back towards Point Pleasant on Route 62. I thought I would drive back through the TNT area since I had not been there since I was little.

Were you familiar with any of the Mothman stories or reports from the 60s?

No. I had briefly heard bits and pieces of the story when I was younger. I really had no ideas as to what it was. It was only just recently that I started reading John Keel's book, and in the back of my mind I started to think maybe what I saw and what happened up there, maybe were related somehow.

Keel wrote about a "zone of fear" or having an uneasy feeling...almost as if someone was watching him or looking over his shoulder.

I knew nothing about any of that.

Did you experience that type of feeling?

I had gone clear back to where the pond that we used to fish in was located. There were several ponds surrounded by trees. The only time I had been back there was when I was 8 or 9 years old with my aunt. That is why I decided to drive back there again. I remember shutting the car off and being there for approximately 10 minutes.

After that I began to sense that something was not quite right. It was just a weird, cold chill type of feeling. I knew something wasn't right and I started to look around. I had never really experienced that feeling before, and haven't since then. Even when I talk about it now, I get a chill going down my back. It was just a weird sense of fear coming on. I remember looking around to see if I could see car lights because I felt like something was there. I felt like we were in a dangerous situation...very uneasy as if something was going to happen.

What time in the evening did this happen?

It was between 9pm and 9:30pm...it was before 10pm. I remember trying to drive around after this happened to shake the whole ordeal off.

So was the other person that was with you at this time shaken by the experience?

The person with me at this time was shaken just from the fact that they knew that I was upset. They could tell that I was obviously very nervous. When I began to feel uncomfortable about the situation, I started the car and proceeded to leave. At that time I was scouting around trying to see something, because I had never sensed that feeling before or ever since then.

Did you hear anything?

I did not hear anything. I am sure I had the tape player on and I don't remember turning it off at that point. I took to the road heading back towards Route 62. It just literally felt like something evil was following me. I started off driving at a fairly normal speed, because I knew the road was straight. I was still scanning around trying to figure out what was going on. I saw this big, bird-looking thing fly over top of my car. I mean it was big. It was every bit of 6 feet tall with a huge wingspan on it.

Can you estimate the size of the wingspan?

I know that it was wider than my car because when it went over it was like gliding so I could see that the wings were much wider than the car. The wings did not move per say but it was like a glide when it went over the car. I saw that and I had no idea what this thing was but I knew that is what it was that I felt. I tromped on the gas and out the road we went. This thing continued several times to go out over the car and then go straight up in the air.

Did this thing get in front of the car at any time?

No. I am guessing that when it went over top of my car each time, it couldn't have been no more than 3 to 5 feet higher than the car. It was so close, it looked like you could have reached out and touched it. It never hit the car. By this time it had flew straight up into the air, and I had really hit the gas and took off. I remember glancing down at the speedometer and I had it pegged. This thing continued to repeatedly come right over us at the exact same height. I was yelling, "Did you see it?" to the other person in the car, and trying to drive at the same time.

At that point they were terrified, too, and cowering down in the seat, but still had not seen this thing flying over us. It stayed over the car all the way out to Route 62, where I took a left turn and headed towards Point Pleasant. I continued trying to look for it while we were on the main road all the way past the Armory, but I never saw it following us at that point.

Did you ever see any red eyes on this thing?

I can't verify seeing red eyes. As fast as this thing was going, it almost looked like it had a yellowish, glowing outline to it. The body of it was dark. When it flew over us, it passed us like we were sitting still. When it would fly straight up, I would lose sight of it, but then it would always loop back down and fly directly above the car.

Many people thought that headlights on the cars were attracting this thing....

For years I tried to convince myself that it was the lights off the airport, but the image of this thing was too plain. I knew that the airport lights would not magically shoot straight up in the air either. I have never had the nerve to go back there. You wouldn't see something like that even in a zoo.

How many times do you estimate that this thing went over the car?

At least 5 or 6 times during the run towards Route 62. I had to have been going up to 120 miles per hour at one point in time, so I cannot imagine how fast that thing was going to do what it was doing. I remember that the wings were not tilting at all. Just perfectly straight and gliding.

Did you think about going to the police after you arrived in Point Pleasant?

No, because they would have thought I was nuts. I guess I was just trying to rationalize the whole experience at that point. I was pretty shaken up, and I remember going down to Krodel Park at about 10pm, and tried to calm down. It's something I will never forget.

ARCHIVES:
The Silver Bridge

Our Worst Bridge Disaster: WHY

While the nation awaits the verdict of the experts seeking clues to one of history's most tragic bridge collapses, we have uncovered the startling story of the controversial engineering features of Silver Bridge across the Ohio, which will answer your concern about bridges you use

By ALDEN P. ARMAGNAC

It was all over in seconds—"a few" to 30, by horrified witnesses' estimates. Silver Bridge at Point Pleasant, W. Va., a two-lane suspension bridge whose three spans totaled 1,460 feet, collapsed from end to end and tower tops to piers—and vanished into the Ohio River. For most of the people in the cars and trucks that jammed it at 4:55 p.m. last December 15, there was no chance of escape.

At least 39 died, in vehicles pitched to the dark-brown water 80 feet below. That

All that was left of Silver Bridge is seen in air view—bare piers in river, tangled girders on far (Ohio) shore. In seconds, rest of bridge and people on it vanished beneath water.

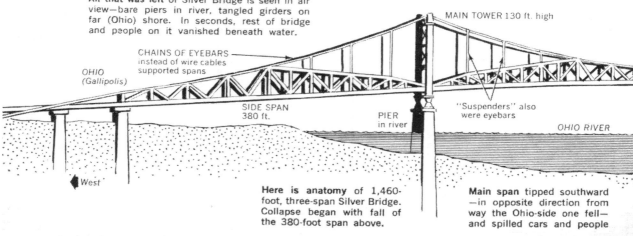

Here is anatomy of 1,460-foot, three-span Silver Bridge. Collapse began with fall of the 380-foot span above.

Main span tipped southward —in opposite direction from way the Ohio-side one fell—and spilled cars and people

Silver Bridge, in foreground, looked like this before it fell. It was a heavily traveled Ohio River highway crossing on U.S. 35, just downstream of a railroad bridge (background) that is still in use. Both this photo and the after-collapse photo on opposite page are from West Virginia side.

DID IT HAPPEN?

was the count by early this year, as divers and floating derricks continued the grim task of hauling up cars to recover bodies within. In toll of lives it looked like the worst U.S. highway-bridge disaster; a search of newspaper files and engineering journals found none before to match it.

What made Silver Bridge fall? Could it happen to the next bridge you drive over?

Overloading was the cause, said Prof. Thomas Stelson, head of the civil engineering department of Carnegie-Mellon University. Others agreed. The 39-year-old bridge was built to less demanding specifications than today's, which allow for the weight of modern tractor-trailers. But a mystery remained. Bridges have fallen before—but for a great steel bridge to fold up all at once and disappear is almost incredible.

President Johnson ordered a federal inquiry into the collapse—and into ways to assure the safety of the nation's other bridges. Additional probes began.

While clue-seekers puzzled over Silver Bridge's wreckage, PS tried delving into its original engineering. The hitherto untold story that resulted was filled with startling surprises.

Continued

Span over Ohio shore tipped northward (to right) and fell on side, battering wrecked cars with debris. By witnesses' accounts, this was the first of bridge's three spans to give way.

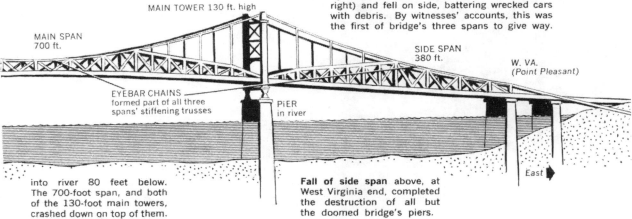

into river 80 feet below. The 700-foot span, and both of the 130-foot main towers, crashed down on top of them.

Fall of side span above, at West Virginia end, completed the destruction of all but the doomed bridge's piers.

Radical features of bridge could have contributed to disaster—and at least

No ordinary bridge, Silver Bridge got its name because it was the country's first aluminum-painted one—but that was the least unusual thing about it. Its design was the very antithesis of conservative. It incorporated at least five radical features—some of them virtually thrust upon the bridge's designers, the J. E. Greiner Co. of Baltimore. Most could have contributed to the disaster, and at least one certainly did. These were the engineering novelties:

Eyebars instead of wire cables. The most conspicuous innovation of Silver Bridge was suspending it from chains of eyebars—instead of conventional suspension-bridge cables, made up of hundreds or thousands of parallel wires.

With its 700-foot main span, it was the first eyebar suspension bridge of its size in the U.S. In all the world, there had been only three large ones, including an eyebar suspension bridge built at Budapest in 1903 and another at Cologne in 1915. The world's largest, with a main span of 1,114 feet, was the Florianopolis Bridge in Brazil—a rail-and-highway bridge completed in 1926, only two years before Silver Bridge, and in many ways its prototype.

Silver Bridge hung on two chains of eyebars. Each link of a chain consisted of two eyebars, side by side. A massive pin, passing through holes in the eyebars' enlarged and slightly thickened ends, joined each link to the next.

A link's two eyebars were supposed to share equally the 4½-million-pound pull on a cable. Some civil engineers, in professional-society discussions, voiced qualms. One eyebar conceivably might get more stress than the other, if it stretched less under tension, or if its pinholes were inadvertently spaced a trifle closer than the other one's.

Beyond dispute, at any rate, was the comment obvious to any layman: *A chain is no stronger than its weakest link.* And the question of how strong and uniform the links actually were brings up the Ohio River bridge's next radical feature:

Novel "high-tension" eyebars. Silver Bridge's eyebars were of heat-treated carbon steel—a new kind, just developed by the American Bridge Co. Their first use anywhere was in the 1926 Brazilian bridge; Silver Bridge was the first in the U.S. to use them. Before that, eyebars had been made of regular structural steel, or of nickel steel.

Eyebars of the new high-tension material, it was claimed, could be subjected to much more stress than had been safe before—with resulting economy in material, weight, and cost. And thereby hangs a curious tale:

Silver Bridge was to have been a wire-cable one. That type was originally recommended by the Greiner firm to the bridge's first owner—a private toll-bridge company, which later sold it to West Virginia. Likewise, a wire-cable design was first chosen for its prototype, the Florianopolis Bridge, by Robinson and Steinman of New York. In both cases that choice was overridden, when the American Bridge Co. convinced the economy-minded clients that an eyebar bridge would be cheaper. The designers had to revamp their plans.

First of the new eyebars made in quantity were the 400-odd for the Bra-

Raising sunken cars, to recover bodies of those killed outright or drowned, came first. Cutting and ripping away wreckage, to reach cars, unavoidably hindered examining it later for disaster clues.

one certainly did

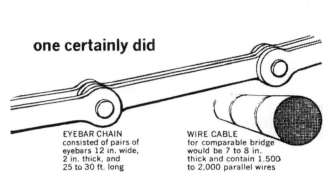

EYEBAR CHAIN consisted of pairs of eyebars 12 in. wide, 2 in. thick, and 25 to 30 ft. long

WIRE CABLE for comparable bridge would be 7 to 8 in. thick and contain 1,500 to 2,000 parallel wires

Chains of eyebars (top), instead of conventional wire cables (below), served to hold up Silver Bridge. It was the first eyebar suspension bridge of its size in this country—and one of few in the world.

zilian bridge. Most were too long for a testing machine to check their quality. How they were made was the company's secret. (It was still experimenting, a spokesman said later.) And the bridge's noted co-designer, Dr. D. B. Steinman, in *Engineering News-Record* for Nov. 13, 1924, made one of the most extraordinary statements ever printed in an engineering journal: His firm declined to take any responsibility for the strength and safety of its bridge's eyebars—which was as much as saying, the safety of its eyebar-suspended bridge.

Designers of Silver Bridge had less reason for misgivings, since its shorter eyebars offered no testing problems—and the company's secrecy about its process had ended by 1927. High-tension eyebars were nevertheless something still regarded as new.

Double duty for eyebars. Silver Bridge's designers added a unique feature by building the eyebar chains into a part of all three spans' stiffening trusses, as top members. Florianopolis Bridge had pioneered in this, but for its center span only; Silver Bridge went it one better.

Due to this feature—and to a tower design to be described—Silver Bridge's structural elements were exceptionally dependent on each other for safety.

Unique anchorages. For lack of bedrock within economical reach, the eyebar chains ended in concrete blocks poured in shallow excavations, around the tops of hundreds of concrete piles. These novel anchorages were the only one of the bridge's radical features positively exonerated of contributing to the disaster; they were found intact afterward.

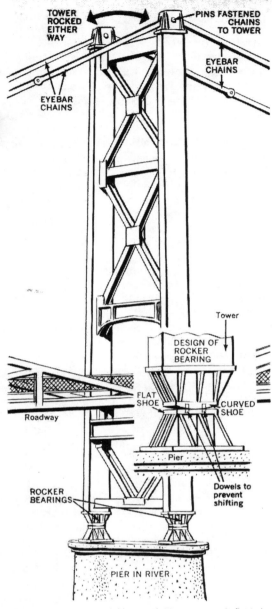

"Rocker" towers of Silver Bridge, one of first in U.S. to have them, swayed freely on curved bases. This provided for movement of eyebar chains, pinned to tops, with varying temperatures and loads. Rocker design, later used widely, was sound and advantageous—but relied on eyebar chains to hold towers up. If the chains broke, or went slack, the rocker towers would fall—and Silver Bridge's towers did.

"Rocker" towers. On the face of it, one innovation—rocker towers—must have contributed to the magnitude of the Silver Bridge tragedy.

For comparison, rigid towers of masonry or steel supported our earliest large suspension bridges. The towers'

[*Continued on page 188*]

Our Worst Bridge Disaster
[Continued from page 105]

saddles for cables were on rollers to permit the cables' longitudinal and tension-equalizing movement, in response to varying temperatures and loads.

Then came flexible towers—whose bases were fixed, but whose tops could sway with the cables.

Rocker towers, whose introduction was hailed by engineers as the next forward step, are free to rock back and forth with the cables. Instead of having fixed bases, they stand on curved shoes, bearing against flat ones on the piers. Nothing anchors the bottom of a tower—aside from loose-fitting dowels to keep it from shifting. Sliding or rocking connections support the roadway structure, passing through a tower, without hindering the tower's movement.

Silver Bridge was almost the first of its size in the U.S. to have rocker towers. (A wire-cable suspension bridge at Portsmouth, Ohio, preceded it by a year.)

Often used since, rocker towers are sound and advantageous. Importantly, they avoid the strain put on a pier by the bending of a flexible-type tower. This advantage applies especially to medium-size suspension bridges, whose towers lack the inherent flexibility of the biggest bridge's high ones.

However—and this proved a big "however" in Silver Bridge's case—a rocker tower presupposes that the safety of the cables, or eyebar chains, is beyond question. For those are what it depends on to brace it and hold it up.

If Silver Bridge's eyebar chains broke, or went slack from a structural failure elsewhere, down would come the towers. Even a single chain's parting or slacking would be catastrophic. ("If one chain goes, it all goes," comments an Ohio bridge engineer.)

One of these things must have happened—for both towers did fall.

The rocker towers seem to solve the mystery of how Silver Bridge could collapse in seconds, and claim so many lives.

A bridge's fall that was another story. For a contrasting example, take the spectacular collapse in 1940 of the Tacoma Narrows Bridge—then the world's third-longest suspension bridge. Designed too flexibly, it was twisted apart by wind.

Almost all the 2,800-foot main span's suspended structure fell, piecemeal, into waters below. But the five people on the bridge were unhurt. Though damaged, the great cables held; though wrenched and bent, the towers stayed up. And so did the side spans that gave an escape route to safety.

If overloading felled Silver Bridge, and its remarkable design explains the record death toll—and so it appears—all that remains is to reconstruct the details.

Hunting clues. Still unknown at this writing was what gave way first, and the exact sequence of what followed. Best hope of finding out, if ever, lay at a 27-acre plot near the bridge site. There, airplane-crash style, investigators were reassembling wreckage from the shore and river bottom in search of clues.

Lengths of eyebar chains that fell on the Ohio shore were intact. Reportedly under suspicion was a broken eyebar-chain support, at the extreme Ohio end, over which the north eyebar chain made its sharpest bend between tower and anchorage. But it was a formidable problem to distinguish what broke first from what parted later. The study was expected to take a year.

Meanwhile the tragedy is spurring intensive safety checks of bridges all over the nation. West Virginia, for one, began a searching inspection of its 500 major bridges. One in particular, understandably, is getting an extra-special going-over that may take months.

St. Mary's Bridge over the Ohio, some 70 miles upstream from Silver Bridge and built about the same time, is its exact twin—and is believed its only U.S. counterpart. If St. Mary's Bridge proves free of flaws, possibly special limits may be imposed on its traffic's weight and spacing. Discovery of defects calling for the bridge's repair, strengthening, or replacement might throw more light on what happened to Silver Bridge.

What it all adds up to is that you can be reassured about the safety of bridges you'll cross. Not only is the disaster inspiring nationwide precautions, but also —with the sole exception just noted— you'll never encounter another bridge like Silver Bridge.

Charleston Gazette-Mail, Sunday, Dec. 17, 1967

'Eye Bar' — This is the "eye bar" suspension which held the Point Pleasant bridge up—until Friday. The chain linkage (foreground) was Silver Bridge "cable." (Photo by Jack K…)

At right: *Within one week the suggestion was made that the collapse of the Silver Bridge may have been due to something other than mechanical and structural failure.*

Preceding pages: *The March 1968 issue of* Popular Science *looks closely at the engineering failure attributed to the collapse of the Silver Bridge. Special attention in detail was paid to the rocker bearings, which provided no resistance under the strain of one eyebar chain carrying the load of the entire bridge deck. (Courtesy of* Popular Science*)*

Cornstalk's Curse Termed Only Myth

Since last Friday's river catastrophe, rumors have plagued the county that this came about through a curse placed on the area by Shawnee Chief Cornstalk, but Mrs. Holly Simmons who is a member of the West Virginia State Historical Society discounts this by saying it is only a myth.

Mrs. Simmons, who lives on Viand Street, in refuting the rumor of a curse, based her conclusion on research of early history.

However many of those raised in this county had heard the tale since early childhood, but other historians were also quick to discount it.

Apparently this stemmed from the murder of Cornstalk and his son Illinipsico. An account of their death is recorded in a book titled "The Battle of Point Pleasant" by Mrs. Livia Nye Simpson - Poffenbarger.

According to the documents in part: "In the spring of 1777, when the great Indian uprising was again taking place, Cornstalk came to Fort Randolph at Point Pleasant to warn the whties of their danger and was retained as a hostage, during the whole summer."

"... The bravery of Cornstalk called forth the admiration of even his brutal mugderers, as he thus addressed Illinipsico. 'My son, the Great Spirit has seen fit that we should die together, and has sent you here to that end. It is His will and let us submit: it is all for the best!' and then turning his face to his murderers at the door, he fell without a groan pierced with seven bullets."

The next three pages feature a dozen photos of the aftermath of the worst bridge disaster in U.S. history—the collapse of the Silver Bridge. (Photos courtesy of Brian Zeller)

Former Inspector States
Bridge Had Developed Crack Prior to '67

By FRANK T. CSONGOS

CHARLESTON, W. Va. (UPI) — A former inspector's disclosure that the ill-fated Silver Bridge had developed a crack three years before its 1967 collapse highlighted Monday's start of a mamoth claims case filed on behalf of 46 people killed in the disaster.

At stake in the landmark case is the fate of 56 claims, all claiming the West Virginia Department of Highways was negligent in the bridge's failure.

Initially, the case before the Court of Claims involves lawsuits filed on behalf of two victims, and the outcome of the test cases will decide a precedent for all other claims.

Edward Cundiff, a former bridge inspector, who provided the key testimony as the $6.5 million trial began, said he noticed a small fault in the Ohio River span three years before it crumbled, spilling cars and trucks lined in bumper-to-bumper traffic in rush-hour traffic during the Christmas shopping season.

When a heavy truck rolled across the bridge during a 1964 inspection, Cundiff testified he recalled the bridge emitted "a bad vibration," and that it needed some "cleaning and rusting."

Under examination by Chester Lovett, a Charleston attorney representing the estate of James White of Ravenswood, Cundiff acknowledged he did not check the vibration of the bridge during rush hour traffic.

"The most I saw on it were 10 cars and two trucks," Cundiff said.

The structure crumbled during heavy traffic Dec. 15, 1967.

When questioned by Attorney General Chauncey Browning Jr. the chief representative for the state, Cundiff said he did not believe the condition of the bridge was unsafe at the time of his inspection.

Attorneys for the claimants contended the bridge fell into the river because of a crack in its upper structure.

Cundiff, currently a complaint investigator in the Department of Highways, said he made two official inspections of the bridge and reported his findings to the state. But he insisted he crossed the span at least 15 times and undertook periodic unofficial inspections.

"I visited the bridge a week before it fell," he said.

"Waht did you see?" Lovett asked.

"Nothing out of the ordinary" Cundiff replied.

Harry A. Sherman, a Pittsburgh attorney representing the estate of Melvin Cantrell of Point Pleasant, said during the lunch break he believes the claimants have an "airtight case" against the state.

Browning disagreed, however saying the "burden of proving that the state acted negligently" rested with the claimants.

Cantreell and White both perished in the bridge collapse and their estates are seeking damages for wrongful death from the state.

Presiding Judge Henry L. Ducker of Huntington predicted the case could drag on for "several months."

The other two judges on the bench were John B. Garden of Wheeling and W. Lyle Jones of Bridgeport.

If the court rules that the state was not responsible for the disaster, all claims would be disallowed, Browning said.

West Virginia has a $112,000 maximum limit that can be collected for death by a claimant and the legislature then must decide whether to appropriate the money.

Overload Seen Likely Cause Of Bridge Fall

CHARLESTON — A partner in the engineering firm that designed the Silver Bridge said in New York Monday that the structure may have collapsed due to either an overload of traffic or a change in construction plans that had been made 40 years ago to save money.

Edward J. Donnelly, a partner in the J. E. Greiner Co., said the Baltimore firm of consulting engineers that designed the bridge have sent a six-man team of structural engineers to investigate the collapse.

Donnelly said in an interview that the original specifications for the structure called for its use by two-axle trucks weighing 15 tons. He noted that current bridge specifications call for use by three-axle tractor-trailers weighing 36 tons. "These vehicles were not dreamed about when the bridge was designed," he said.

Donnelly's comments on the weight of traffic are confirmed by an article in the Engineering News-Record of June 20, 1929, written by Wilson T. Ballard, then a vice president of the Geiner firm.

"The bridge was designed for an American Society of Civil Engineers H-15 (15-ton) loading, and all bids were submitted on this live-load requirements," Ballard wrote. The article also pointed out that the bridge was the first of its type to be built in the United States.

The design incorporated the use of eyebar rather than twisted wire cables, as stiffening trusses for the 700-foot-long center span and the two 380-foot-long side spans.

"The original design called for wire cables spun in place in the conventional manner," the article said but the design "was changed although the reason for alteration in plans is not immediately clear.

Donnelly said his firm originally had recommended cables rather than eyebars. Asked the reason for the change, he said: "One can only presume that eyebars were cheaper." He added that the use of eyebars in bridge construction ended in the 1930's.

Donnelly said he could not visualize metal fatigue as a reason for collapse because it was a constant tension support system with "no reversal of stress" that could lead to metal fatigue.

As to vibration as a cause, Donnelly said if this were the reason, it should have shown up on inspection long ago.

When the Greiner Company designed the bridge and supervised its construction, the steel superstructure was erected by the American Bridge Co., a subsidiary of the United States Steel Corp.

Donnelly said eyebars were a copyrighted design of the American Bridge Co. George Hess, a spokesman for the firm in New York, said the company's offices were unaware that the Point Pleasant bridge had been built by American Bridge. He said records would have to be checked to determine why the eyebar system was used instead of cable.

An early headline announces the grim news of the Silver Bridge tragedy.

```
Case Number: WV-35559-109M
WITNESS NAME: CURT CLONCH

Sighting Report: Kanauga, OH
Description: Silver Bridge Collapse
Report Date: December 15, 1967
```

A Case of Campbell's Soup

Little did Curt Clonch realize that his typical day working at Tiny's grocery store at the foot of the Silver Bridge in Ohio would be a day he would never forget. It was a cold, chilly morning on December 15th, 1967 when Curt headed out for work to cross the Silver Bridge. It would be the last time he would ever cross it. Only minutes before he would begin his 5 pm trek back over to Point Pleasant he would witness the massive, steel structure twist and tumble into the cold, icy waters of the Ohio River. Curt's eyewitness account of the tragic events on that day gives us a firsthand look at the terrifying moments leading up to this disaster of gigantic magnitude, the collapse of the Silver Bridge.

It is important to remember that forty six innocent lives perished that December day. This was no Hollywood stunt or something made up for television or a movie. It was an event that changed the people of Point Pleasant forever and many other neighboring river towns as well. Curt Clonch will tell you that it changed his life too.

I wanted to ask you about that terrible day on December 15, 1967. You worked at a grocery store directly at the foot of the bridge on the Ohio side of the river?

My wife and I lived in Henderson, West Virginia, and she was pregnant at the time with our oldest daughter. It was a very cold morning and I had gotten up at around 7 am and I had to be at the store by 8 am. I worked at Tiny's Foodland (note: no direct connection with Tiny's Drive-in located in upper Point Pleasant near 30th Street). I usually crossed the Silver Bridge twice a day and sometimes three times if I came home for lunch. On that particular morning on the 15th of December we talked about going out to buy a Christmas tree after I left work. I told my wife that I would try and clock out early to leave work. I left for work and worked all day and I remember the store being very busy that day because of the upcoming holiday rush. I have told people that what saved my life that day was a case of Campbell's soup. I normally got off work at 5 pm but at about 4:50 pm I went back to the office and clocked out and started up towards the middle aisle of the store. Normally I would walk up the outside wall inside the store and then would cross the store and go out the front door but on that particular day I walked up the aisle that had all of the canned goods and the soup display. I don't know why. I had already clocked out and as I walked up the aisle I noticed that the soup display was empty. I thought it would be a good idea to run back and get more soup since we had been so busy in the store and the soup was on sale. We were running the soup on sale for 5 cents a can. I walked back into the stockroom and picked up two cases of Campbell's soup and brought it out. I remember cutting the cardboard facing off of the front of the boxes and just slid them in the shelf. I heard a rumbling sound and I heard one of the clerks up front say something about the bridge. I ran up towards the front of the store and ran out onto the front porch and loading area covered by an awning. I walked out there and saw that bridge. When I got out there the bridge was still intact but it was weaving and bouncing up and down. It looked like it was moving up and down about 2 or 3 feet right in the middle section of the bridge. As I stood there looking from the Ohio side towards the Point Pleasant side I watched the bridge tilt towards my right and dropped down about 4 to 6 feet. It went down and then sprang right back up. When it sprang back up to where it was about level or even then it gave two or three times more. After that happened I watched the two towers that were holding the concrete span up just fold inwards towards one another. I thought to myself, *Oh my*. It was just unbelievable what I was seeing. There were dump trucks on top of the bridge along with semi-trailers and cars.

Upon closer inspection one can see Tiny's Grocery store located at the foot of the Kanauga, Ohio ramp of the Silver Bridge. Store employee Curt Clonch watched in horror as the Silver Bridge collapsed during evening rush hour on December 15, 1967. (Courtesy of Brian Zeller)

Was the traffic backed up because of the signal lights located at the foot of each end of the bridge?

The traffic was backed up coming across to Ohio and it was backed up going towards Point Pleasant because at that time that was the main traffic route from Columbus on Route 35 heading to Charleston, West Virginia. From the Ohio side I could see that the traffic was backed up past the first pier and since it was rush hour on a Friday evening it

was busy. When the towers tilted towards one another the deck of the bridge just broke in two. Trucks, cars and all just went into the water and then the towers fell right behind them. When it hit the water it shot a stream of water up in the air probably 50 to 75 feet high. Then there was just an eerie silence all around. I heard people screaming so I ran down and crossed the highway and walked up onto the remaining part of the bridge ramp. I was one of the first people there. Everyone on the land side was not hurt because they had gotten out of their cars and ran down the sidewalk of the bridge to safety. I remember one particular car that was sitting right where the bridge broke off and the back wheels of the car were dangling in mid air. There were vehicles lying on the concrete but most of those people were not seriously injured but very shaken up. I then ran over towards the river bank and I could see some people out there in the river holding on to anything that was floating. City Ice and Fuel had a fuel dock on the Point Pleasant side near the floodwall and by the time I made it to the river they had already brought out their tugboat and were on their way to the center of the river to rescue the people that were floating or hanging on to things. All of that happened within approximately 2 to 3 minutes, it was about 3 minutes till 5 pm. Normally I would have gone ahead and got in my car and left the store and been on top of that bridge. For some reason it just wasn't my time to go I guess.

Was there much noise when the bridge began to collapse?

Oh yes. It sounded like a whole line of jets flying over top, almost a deafening sound and rumble. It was making a cracking and popping sounds and the cables were snapping. It was screeching and twisting and just making a terrible sound. It seemed to me like a long time but it couldn't have been more than 2 or 3 minutes total for the whole thing to fall into the river. Everything just disappeared. All you could see now was just the two concrete piers standing on each side of the river. When the bridge hit the water there was some churning but then it was finally just very calm. If you would have walked up there and looked at it you couldn't tell that there was ever a bridge there other than seeing all the debris on land.

Do you remember hearing any time of a sonic boom or a noise as if the sound barrier had been broken when the bridge collapsed?

I heard what sounded like a jet flying very low to ground but not quite as loud and the sound barrier being broken. It was a very loud rumble.

You drove across the Silver Bridge daily. Do you recall what kind of shape or condition the bridge was in at that time?

The Saturday before the bridge fell I had left work and went home and we came back across the bridge. When we crossed the bridge I told my wife that it felt like it was moving. It always gave and moved before when we had been on it but on this day it seemed like it was moving more than it normally did. She crossed the bridge after that with her parents and her dad was teasing her about the bridge moving up and down. A week later the bridge was gone. From looking at that bridge you would have never thought that there anything wrong with it.

What happened next as the shock of the tragedy began to finally sink in?

After I ran down to the river I knew that there little that I could do to help. I had checked on the people that were on the land section of the bridge and they were shaken up but were all doing okay. I ran back to the store and went into the office and started to call my wife on the telephone. When I picked up the phone, I couldn't call out. There were all kinds of voices on the phone because people were trying to call into the store and the telephone line had become overloaded. You could literally hear people talking on there. I hung up the phone and ran out to my car and drove down the road to a gas station. There were people there so I bypassed that and went on down to a Sunoco station. I told the man working there that the Silver Bridge had just fallen. He said, "You're lying." I told him that I needed to call home and before I knew it he just took off and left the station unattended. I called my wife and I told her that I was okay and that I would be home in a few minutes. I didn't tell her that the bridge had collapsed because I didn't want to upset her and possibly cause her to go into labor. After I hung up then she heard on the radio about the bridge falling. Naturally she thought that I had called her before I was going to cross the bridge. She ran about 3 blocks to her parents' house and told her mother that she couldn't remember if I had called her before or after the bridge had fallen. It was now about 5:15 pm and when I tried to call her back I could not get her to answer the phone. I had to drive to Pomeroy, Ohio, and cross over to Mason, West Virginia, to get back down to Point Pleasant. The trip took well over an hour and all that time she didn't know what had happened to me. It was just a terrible, terrible time. I can see and hear in my mind right now that bridge falling and even if I live to be 100 years old it is something I will never forget.

Just a year prior to the bridge disaster the Mothman and UFO sightings were happening here in Point Pleasant. What are your memories of that?

I graduated in 1964 from P.P.H.S. and my wife graduated in 1965 and it was taking place shortly after that. The first thing I did was jumped in my vehicle and headed for TNT because I wanted to see this thing. You couldn't get into the TNT area because of all the traffic backed up all the way down Route 62. I wanted to get up there and see what it looked like. My wife was friends with Linda Scarberry and we knew all of the other kids that saw it because we went to school with all of them. They were a good bunch of kids and we didn't believe they had any reason to make that stuff up or to lie about anything. I remember talking to them about that thing chasing them in their car and why they didn't stop to get a better look at it. My wife and I went up the TNT area like everyone else to see it but we never saw the Mothman. I do know about the Silver Bridge. I do know that for a fact because I watched it fall.

An early photo of the Silver Bridge looking from the Ohio side towards Point Pleasant, West Virginia. Note the absence of the Point Pleasant floodwall at the time the picture was taken. (Courtesy of Brian Zeller)

Illustration by Michael Gray/Courtesy Chad Lambert

```
Case Number: WV-35559-110M
WITNESS NAME: LAWRENCE GRAY

Sighting Report: At Home/Point Pleasant, WV
Description: Six-Foot Glowing Apparition
Report Date: August 1966
```

Visions of Mothman?

One perspective on the Mothman encounters from some witnesses I have interviewed leans towards an apparition of evil or some foreboding sense of spiritual imagery. Lawrence Gray found himself lying in his bed wide awake at 3 am one morning in the fall of 1966 at his home in Point Pleasant. What he described standing inside of his bedroom that morning certainly qualifies for the unexplainable and obviously disturbs Mr. Gray even today when he speaks about it. While many of my investigations center on the physical element it was important to find witnesses who have seen what they describe as more than a physical object or being. Lawrence Gray's detailed account will possibly explain that the Mothman was not always a figure or creature that you could reach out and touch but a vision of something terrible.

You went to school here in Point Pleasant?

Correct. I graduated from Point Pleasant High School in 1960.

So you were living here when all of the Mothman sightings were taking place? What was your personal opinion at that time about all that was happening here in Point Pleasant?

Well, when I first heard about it, I thought it was probably a large bird of some sort. After I saw whatever I saw my thoughts changed about it.

Can you give me a time frame of your experience?

Yes. It was in the fall of 1966. I left for Frankfurt, Indiana, in September, 1966, so this had to have been around August of that year.

Tell me about what happened.

I lived on Jefferson Avenue across from what is now the Wesleyan church. It was a little white house across the street. My wife and I were renting it at the time. I was working in Middleport, Ohio, at a supermarket as a meat department manager. My wife and I were thinking about going to Bible College in Indiana. So we were living in this little house, and I was a member of the Pilgrim Holiness church, which was also located across the street from our house. I would go over to the church every morning and have my devotions, and pray or read my Bible, before I would go to work. We were attending a revival service at the church during that time.

I remember leaving the church that evening with my wife. It was a nice evening and we crossed Jefferson Avenue and walked towards our house. We walked upon the steps (pauses and describes how he gets chill bumps even now when talking about this) and I immediately sensed that someone had been, or was in, the house. I just had that feeling. This was around 9:30 in the evening. I didn't mention this to my wife, because I figured she would think I was joking. So I opened the front door and we went into the house, and the feeling became much stronger to me that something just was not right. I remember glancing across the living room and I didn't see anything out of place, so I then walked in towards the bathroom.

When you walked through the hall the bathroom was straight ahead, and there was a bedroom on each side of the bathroom. My next response was to go into the bedroom on the side of Jackson Avenue. I looked in the closet and under the bed, and didn't see anything but I still felt that feeling. I didn't let my wife see what I was doing as I checked out the other bedroom. I went into the kitchen and walked towards the back door, with a basement door next to the back door. We always kept a little hook-style lock on that basement door, so we would know if anyone had been in the basement.

I noticed that the lock was unhooked and I thought maybe I had forgotten to lock it. I still had a weird feeling about it, so I went down into the basement to see if there someone down there. I cautiously opened the basement door and turned on the light. I couldn't really see all around the basement. To be honest, about I really didn't want to go down there, but I started down the steps and there was a pipe lying close to the steps, so I picked it up and proceeded on down to the basement. I looked all around but still did not see anything. I headed back upstairs, but I still had that same feeling that I had when we came into the house.

Was this feeling you are describing a feeling of fear?

It was. It was dread, fear, a sense that there was somebody there and I couldn't see them. So the evening went on, and finally we went to bed at around 10:30 or 11:00 pm. Our bedroom faced Jefferson Avenue and the foot of my bed did also. I slept on the window side. I was lying there in bed, and all of a sudden, I found myself awake and looking out the window. I remember all of this very clearly.

The Church of God was down on the corner, and a bright street light was out in front of that church. A car pulled up there and stopped and then went on down the street. I remember looking at the car and wondering, *Why am I awake?* I didn't feel anything at that moment.

I turned my head back across that bed, and there this thing stood. It just sort of paralyzed me and I was frozen with fear. I was taken by what I was seeing, and I was really afraid at this point. It was standing there and I tried to yell, but I couldn't make a noise. My wife was lying right beside of me asleep. This thing was standing there, and it was at least six feet tall, maybe a little taller from where I was laying. It was sort of a dirty, lunar color and it had some sort of a glowing look to it.

The glow was not illustrious, but it did glow somewhat. It had places for eyes, but I couldn't see any eyes, because they were kind of back in the head area. This thing could see me, and I could see it, even though I couldn't see pupils or eyes, but we both knew we were looking at each other (sighs and shrugs while sitting in chair). To me, I am convinced as sure as I am sitting in this chair, that this was the devil.

Illustration by Derek Clark

At this time most of the Point Pleasant sightings of the Mothman and UFOs had really not even taken place yet.

No. This would have been a couple months before that started.

Many witnesses described a winged creature…did you notice any wings or arms?

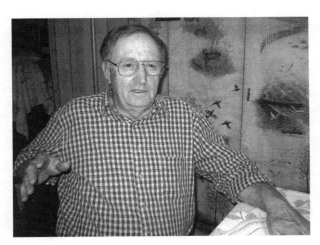

Alright, this thing had two arms — or things that looked like wings — and it was standing like this (demonstrates a figure standing with shoulders shrugged and head tilted). I did not see any red eyes of any sort. I believe that the devil is able to manifest himself as an angel of light or anything he wants to. He can be beautiful or he can be ugly.

Did it make any sound at all?

No. But you could sure feel it. You just knew

Illustration by Ron Lanham

that it was communicating that it was this awful being or something. I just seized and froze when I saw it.

How long did you stand there at look at this thing?

I would estimate this lasted for about 45 seconds or so. It went on for awhile. I really didn't know what to do. But when I started thinking of Scripture in my mind, it was just like a slug, it kind of dissipated, not real fast but just sort of went into nothing.

So your wife never woke up or heard anything?

No. She never had a clue. I woke her up and told her, of course, after this thing was gone.

What did she think it could have been?

She thought the same thing that I did. If you read the Bible, and you believe the Bible, then you know that things like this are real. I believe that the devil has to manifest himself in some sort of form or another.

Do you believe that some of the sightings that followed later that year were somehow related to what you encountered, and do you think what you saw was more spiritual or physical in form?

What I saw was physical but it had a spiritual application. I am putting a spiritual interpretation to this because I don't know any other way to explain it. When I went to New Guinea for eight years to do missionary work, I discovered that they have a lot of things like this that goes on over there. They have different names for the exact same thing that I experienced in different parts of the country and provinces. They believe in this type of thing more than people do in this country and it is very much a part of their lives.

Did anything click with you personally when you heard about the TNT area sightings a few months later? Did you feel there was a connection of any kind?

Yes. I didn't say anything about it because again I felt it was just another manifestation of the devil.

Did you ever speak with any of the other witnesses or law enforcement at that time?

No sir. To me it wasn't a law enforcement thing; I saw it as a spiritual manifestation, and, what could they have done?

Going back to your description, you said it was 6 to 7 feet tall and grayish in color. Were there any noticeable facial features of any type?

Just that it had a shape. It had a head and those deep eyes and it was pronounced in its own way. It really wasn't a human form, but it was in the form of a body. The head was very much a head with a wing formation off to its sides. I can see it in my mind just as clear as it was that night.

MOTHMAN? — In a picture taken in August 1967, from left, Roger Dingey, Jeff Hart and David Hudnall pose with what wildlife officials at the time said was a "rare South American vulture." The bird, whose wingspan measured five to six feet, was found inside a cave near New Haven, W.Va. Descriptions of the bird are similar to reported sightings of Mothman. (Submitted photo)

Illustration by Patrick Trisler

UPDATE:
Point Pleasant Today

Former site of the North Power Plant.

The TNT area as it appears today.

Driving towards where the onramp to the Silver Bridge once stood, at Sixth and Main Streets in downtown Point Pleasant. Mary Hyre's former office is just out of view to the immediate right in this photo.

Route 62 heading into Point Pleasant, the scene of the high-speed chase involving the original eyewitnesses and a giant, birdlike man with wings.

Downtown Point Pleasant

Mothman depicted in stainless steel by sculptor Bob Roach of New Haven, West Virginia. Standing at the intersection of Fourth and Main Streets in Point Pleasant, the statue attracts visitors from around the world.

Carolin Harris, known to many for her community involvement in downtown Point Pleasant, has owned and operated her diner for over thirty-five years. The diner inspired the small-town coffee shop atmosphere depicted in the movie version of The Mothman Prophecies.

Illustration by Gary Gibeaut

```
Case Number: WV-35559-111M
WITNESS NAME: FAYE DEWITT

Sighting Report: TNT Area--North Power Plant
Description: Flying Birdlike Man
Report Date: November 1966
```

TNT Area--Mothman's Lair

Late one fall evening in November 1966 Faye Dewitt along with her brothers and sisters enjoyed a night of fun and entertainment at the local drive-in theater in nearby Kanauga, Ohio. They had all heard about the stories at school and around Point Pleasant about the winged Mothman supposedly stalking the grounds up at the local TNT area and her brother was adamant in proving to them that it was nothing more than a hoax or some pranksters. Shortly after the movie ended the carload of kids proceeded towards the TNT area to have a quick look for themselves. It was a night that Faye vividly remembers as one of horror and surprise as they themselves encountered a creature that looked like nothing they had ever seen before. Faye Dewitt was another Mothman witness that was passed over by the press at the time of the major sightings, probably because at that time she was just fourteen years old. In the following interview Faye talks candidly and in great detail about what she and the others saw that November night.

What are your thoughts on the Silver bridge collapse? Most of the Mothman sightings stopped after the collapse.

We were supposed to be on the bridge that day. We went over to Ohio faithfully every Friday. My daddy had to go over to Burris grocery in Kanauga. It had been raining, sleeting and snowing all day long and very cold and he came home from work and he wanted to go on over to get our groceries...never failed. It was so bad that Friday and he kept saying, "Get ready and we'll go." And I said, "Daddy, I really don't want to go out in that mess, that's awfully bad." I said, "The roads were icy and we have enough stuff here to last us at least until tomorrow, and then maybe we can go over tomorrow afternoon after the weather clears up a little bit better." He said, "If it snows bad, we won't be able to get over there." And I said, "We'll still be okay until the evening, and then if we have to we can go somewhere."

I just did not want to go out for some reason. I just felt that something was going to happen. I didn't know what. I felt more like we were going to be involved in a wreck. Daddy kept telling me to get ready and I remember telling him we would be okay until tomorrow. This was around 2 or 3 o'clock in the afternoon. Around 6 o'clock he turned on the news, and that's when it came on that the bridge had fell and I couldn't believe it. He said, "You kept us from being on that bridge. We could have been on there." The main reason I didn't want to go out was because the weather was so bad.

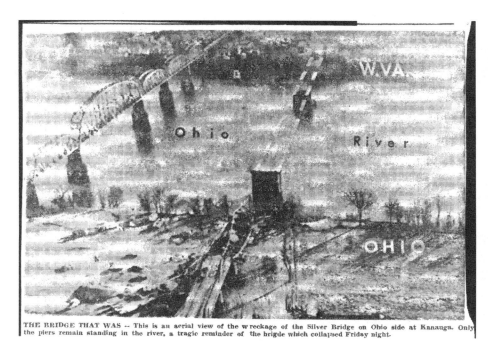

THE BRIDGE THAT WAS -- This is an aerial view of the wreckage of the Silver Bridge on Ohio side at Kanauga. Only the piers remain standing in the river, a tragic reminder of the brigde which collapsed Friday night.

Do you believe the Mothman sightings had anything to do with the bridge collapse?

My own personal opinion is that the government went out to TNT area and caught whatever it was, and they took it out of there and that's why the sightings stopped. I really personally believe they got whatever was out there. I believe they knew exactly what that thing was and what happened to it, and that's why the Mothman sightings stopped. For about two weeks they surrounded the area and wouldn't let anyone up there. That's when they said they had caught the "crane." That made everyone who had seen it mad. Then people began talking about all the chemicals up there and it was possibly some sort of mutation or something that a bird or animal got into.

Do you think that after the intial sightings, people were trying scare everyone who were up there looking for whatever this thing was? Dressing up in costume or something?

Yes...because that's what we thought it was. There is no way no human could run that fast. I don't know of any bird that can without bobbing up and down. It had no beak. It had a feature just like a face. It had a little nub for a nose, with a little bridge that stuck out, and you could see its nostrils. It had a mouth, but if it had any teeth, I never saw them. Its head was shaped like a human's head, but it was all in like feathers, surrounded by them like a dog or a cat.

You claim that the red eyes were very noticeable?

Yes, that's what got me. I turned around and there it was, looking right at me and those eyes were a red you can't describe. They were almost a ruby red.

Some witnesses claim they looked almost like red reflectors, possibly off of a bike or a car.

Yes...kind of like that...almost like a traffic red light. It wasn't a glowing red that would glow in the dark, but it was red that every bit of it showed up. You didn't see anything but those red eyes...that's all I could see.

So after you all saw this creature did you all dwell on what you had seen? Did this affect your life in any way?

We all hashed it out, and tried to figure out what we had seen, and what we thought it was. We talked about it and what everyone was saying they has also saw up there. There is no way I can tell you what it was. In my opinion, I don't believe it was something from another planet. It could have been, because I can't explain how it could travel like that, and just jump up on a building that high.

And that was a three story building.

Yeah, I thought it was about four stories tall.

Illustration by Gary Gibeaut

And there was no type of rooftop access to the North Power Plant at that time.

No, there was not...it was perched up on the top of the building, holding its legs just looking at us. When the chunk of coal my brother threw at it hit not far from its feet, and rolled down that metal roof, that is when it stood up, turned and then just jumped down, off the side of that building. It went up the front first, and then it came down the side of the roof, and basically ran right along beside the car.

So it chased you down the main road going to the fairgrounds, and then when the car pulled in and stopped, you saw it run up to the roof of the North Power plant?

Yes...then we turned off the main road, and then we turned up into the loading dock area. When we were going towards the loading dock area, it was running right beside of the car. That's when I told my brother to speed up. He sped up, but it didn't do any good, so he slammed on the brakes because we couldn't go up into the loading area because the two buildings were sitting so close together we didn't know if it was a dead end road or not. He then spun the car around and put it in an angle, that's when it jumped on the hood of the car.

And then it jumped up on the roof of the North Power Plant?

Yes. It jumped up onto the front side if the building, and sat there and watched us. My brother threw a rock and it hit really close to its feet — that's when it jumped down from the side, and ran and jumped over some large hedges located out from the building.

What happened after it jumped down from the building and you began to drive away in the car?

That was the last we saw of it. We turned around and just went back the way we had came in.

You then drove to the Mason County Sheriff's office in downtown Point Pleasant?

Yes. We drove straight to the courthouse. My brother got out of the car and went down into the basement, and then he returned to the car with the deputy, and he stood and talked to us and wrote everything we told him down.

> ATHENS, OHIO, FRIDAY, NOVEMBER 18, 1966   Ohio River Valley   TEN CENTS
>
> ## Monster No Joke For Those Who Saw It

Was there any doubts about going to the authorities or police — did you think that they may not believe your story?

I left that up to my brother, since he was the one driving and that's where we went to.

What can you say to some of the people that believe this was a hoax or someone dressed up in a costume?

Well, that's what my brother initially thought it was, but all I can say is that he got fooled. He was taking all of us out there so he could prove that it wasn't real. He saw it, and he knew that there was no way that could have been anything human — and it couldn't have been a bird. He was driving, and all I know is that we were going fast and I just remember looking over to my right, and it was right there running beside me.

How close do you think its face was to the glass of the passenger window?

It was very close. It was running alongside the car and there was no room for it to open up any wings or anything, and it could have easily touched the window.

Did you see its arms moving?

I can't really say what its arms were doing. I remember its arms being in front of it.

And you were the first person riding in the car to notice it running beside you?

Yes. At first I thought I was seeing my brother's reflection in the window, so I took another look at it, and when I looked at my brother he looked back to see why I was looking at him...then we both were looking at it in the window. None of the others really saw it until I screamed and was panicking. I was hitting my brother on the leg and telling him to drive faster. We told everyone to get down in the floor and cover their heads.

Red Eyed 'Winged Monster' Sighted in W. V

Did they see the creature when it was on top of the North Power Plant?

My sister Betty saw it, but she was lying over top of my two other brothers, Ray and Jack, who were curled up and crying...so they didn't see it...but Betty raised up and saw it. It was just crouching down up there, almost like a gargoyle, holding its ankles, watching us.

Do you remember the exact time frame as to when you encountered whatever this was?

I remember it being kind of chilly, like in the fall. I know we had just went over the Kanauga drive-in and saw a movie about a white horse. After the movie was over, my brother Carlisle (nicknamed Topper) said we should ride over to TNT area to see what people were seeing there. Just a few days before, in school, we had heard about some people who had seen it, so we decided to ride up there and look around for ourselves. My brother told us it was just someone in a Halloween costume trying to scare everyone.

So you had already heard or read about the sightings in the newspaper?

No, it hadn't came out in the papers yet. We had only heard about it in school, and we had really only heard about it a day or two before we went to the movie that evening. It was about 10pm when we went up there. My brother had just gotten his driver's permit, so he was around 16 years old, and I would have been 14.

Did you drive out the road towards the fairgrounds and then past the North Power Plant?

Well, at that time there were no paved roads out there. The road that turns off the left towards the North Power Plant was a dirt road. That is where we turned and we were going down that road, when in no time that thing was running right beside the car on the passenger side where I was sitting. I didn't know what it was, and at first I thought it was a reflection in the window. Sometimes you can see the reflection of the driver in the window, so I looked at my brother first and then looked

Illustration by Aric Slater

back out the window. That is when it looked at me, and I saw those red eyes.

Right when I saw it, my brother saw it. We were going pretty fast on the road which was all gravel at that time and it was running right beside of us. I kept yelling, "Speed up!" to my brother and remember hitting him on the leg several times to get him to drive faster. We then were driving towards the North Power Plant and the two small loading dock structures. At that time we didn't know of any other exit that we could take to get away from whatever this was. When my brother turned the curve to go towards the North Power Plant, he was going so fast that the car skidded and the rear end of the car slid around, which caused the car to stop and sit angled in the curved section of the road.

When he did this that thing jumped on the hood of the car and squatted down and looked directly at him and me right through the windshield. It then stood up and jumped down took off running and *jumped* — not flew — jumped upon the roof of the North Power Plant and sat there upon the roof holding its knees like this (demonstrates body position), sitting there looking at us.

My brother got out of the car, and picked up a piece of coal from the road and was trying to hit it, to see if it would come back down or move from the rooftop, because he couldn't believe it got up there. He was trying to make it fly or do something, so he was throwing these pieces of coal at it and he threw one big chunk and it hit real close to its feet and started rolling down. When this happened it stood up.

I yelled, "Get back in here...that thing is going to come after us! Get back in here!" So when it stood up, my brother saw where it was getting ready to do something, and he got back into the car. It stood up and turned, and then jumped down from that building again and ran right by our car. There were some big hedges there grown up, and were not trimmed or anything, probably about 5 or 6 feet tall. That thing jumped up over those hedges, and as it got on top of the hedges, that is when it opened up its wings and flew off. It was dark and we couldn't see anything else of it. We waited around for a few minutes to see if it was going to come back, but everyone was pretty upset. I was crying and my brothers in the backseat were crying. We were all telling my brother who was driving to hurry up and get us out of there. Finally he said, "Well, I don't know what it was, but that isn't anyone in a costume." So we left right after that. I don't know what it was we saw up there to this day.

We drove straight downtown to the courthouse in Point Pleasant, and a deputy walked out to the car after my brother went in to tell them what we had seen. He took down all of our information, and all that we said, but I still think to this day he brushed us off as just a bunch of kids. I don't know if anything was ever done with our report, but he told us we were the fifth group of people that had been there reporting a sighting, and he said they would have to do something about it because too many people were beginning to see it. He then asked us if we knew any of the other people who had reported seeing it. We told him that we didn't. He thought we knew these people and had gotten the description from them or maybe were involved in a big joke or something.

Everyone I have ever interviewed always said that the red eyes were hypnotic.

I didn't look at them long enough for them to be hypnotic, but they were the biggest, reddest eyes I've ever seen. They were big and went up to a little point (describes using hands). Great big in the center and then narrow towards the sides.

So whatever this was scared you to the point where you were upset?

Yes, it sure did. Because I didn't know what it was. There is no human that can run alongside a car like that. I don't care if you're doing 30 or 40 miles per hour. It just can't be done.

So do you think this was some sort of bird or some kind of a creature?

That's what made us all so mad, is when it came out in the newspapers that it was a Sandhill crane. That really made us mad and we went and called the police station, and got onto them about it because a crane has a long, skinny neck and long legs and what we saw did not have anything like that. What we saw had a human form. It almost like a short, chunky child form. It had whitish, tan-like feathers like an owl would have.

Linda Scarberry described it as having "angel-like" wings.

Yes, it had very big wings that opened up like a bird. I remember when they opened up they had a very big wingspan.

Did it make any audible sounds at all?

If it did, I don't remember any. The only bird-like features it had were the wings and the feather appearance, almost a tan and white color mixed together. But it did not have a long neck or long, skinny legs like a Sandhill crane. To me it had the head and the body of a chunky child. It had little hands with a claw-like appearance. I saw the hands as it was running beside our car.

How tall was it?

I would say a little over 5 feet tall. It didn't seem to be very tall to me.

Can you describe it's mannerisms when it ran — was it a clumsy runner?

No. It ran very smoothly right beside of the car.

Did it ever hit the car?

No. It was just running and looking in and watching us. You would have thought it would have hit the car, but it didn't. It couldn't have been flying, because it was too close to the door to open up its wings. When it jumped up onto the hood of the car, all I saw was its head and its hands. I didn't notice if its wings were on its back. All I could see was just a figure of something crouching on the hood of the car and looking directly at us.

Were the eyes glowing in any way?

I don't recall them glowing, but they were a deep ruby red. All of the eyes were red. There was no white or anything.

At any time did you think it was going to harm you or anyone in the car?

No. We never thought of that at all. I think the biggest fear, more than anything, was not really knowing what this thing was. I never felt like it was going to do anything to us. We had never seen anything like it.

You said that when the creature went towards the top of the North Power Plant, that it basically jumped and not flew?

It jumped. I did not see any wings open up until it flew towards the top of that building. That's when I saw that it had wings. It had a very big set of wings. It looked like someone unfolding a fan. That's the way it opened up.

Do you remember anything about the presence of any the Men in Black here in Point Pleasant during the Mothman and UFO sightings?

My brother remembers more about that than I do. I do remember the FBI or some other government agency had fenced off the TNT area for about two weeks, and then they announced that they had caught it, and it was a crane or bird of some sort and that made everyone mad, so they retracted it from the papers.

The Sandhill crane theory always pops up in all of the Mothman sightings. Linda Scarberry told me that what she saw was not a bird of any type. So you are saying that what you saw was not a bird?

No. It did not look like any bird. It ha[d] birdlike wings and feathers, almost a sand and white mixed together in its color appearance.

Do you remember the owl that was shot, and people claimed that that was what people were seeing?

Illustration by Gary Gibeaut

Yes. They had pictures of it in the papers. Well, that was not it. That was not what we saw.

Hunt Continues For Monster

ARCHIVES:
Popular Media

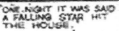

Courtesy of Patrick Trisler

Illustration by J. Carr/Courtesy Allan Gross

Illustration by Jason Moser/Courtesy of Chad Lambert

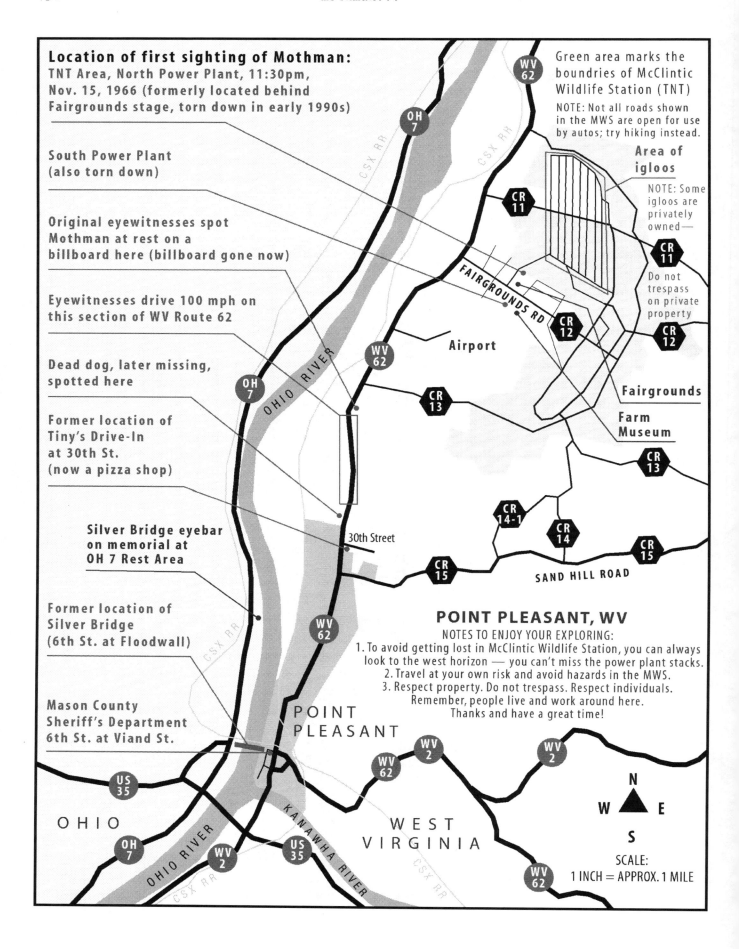

Epilogue

Many people ask me if the final chapter on the Mothman has been written. My answer is a resounding **no**. The interviews and information that I have brought before you, in this book and the previous one, only begin to scratch the surface of this incredible phenomenon of the Mothman. I still revert back to my "iceberg theory" that suggests that only a small portion of this story has been told and that more key eyewitness accounts will hopefully see the light of day. The scientific theories and opinions of so-called "experts" who feel it is their job to tell people what they saw will never cease, just as the steady stream of people who will continue to come forth with more vital information and data. My presentation would not be complete without the sincere, courageous testimonials of the people who have confided in me their trust and honesty, and who without a doubt have brought forth many new angles on what really happened here in Point Pleasant, West Virginia. It is my hope that you continue to search for the truth yourselves, and that my efforts may help you in your own investigations.

— *Jeff Wamsley*

About the Author

Jeff Wamsley is a native of Point Pleasant, West Virginia. He is a graduate of Point Pleasant High School (class of 1980), and also a graduate of the University of Rio Grande, Rio Grande, Ohio (B.A., Art and Design, 1985). A lover of music and and the guitar, Jeff is both a performer and a teacher. He has recorded two albums with his longtime band, **Annex** (*Breaking Ground*, 1987, and *Powers That Be*, 1990).

Jeff founded Criminal Records, a chain of independent record stores, in 1989. He also owns and operates *MothmanLives.com*, a website dedicated to the legend.

Mothman: The Facts Behind the Legend (Mothman Lives Publishing, 2002), which Jeff co-authored with Donnie Sergent, Jr., is a collection of pictures, clippings, and interviews with eyewitnesses to the Mothman phenomenon. It reached #27 on the Amazon.com "Hot 100 Bestsellers List" in February, 2002.

He is also co-founder, along with Carolin Harris, of the annual Point Pleasant Mothman Festival, and is the curator of The World's Only Mothman Museum, located in downtown Point Pleasant, and found online at *mothmanmuseum.com*.

Jeff resides just outside Gallipolis, Ohio, with his wife, Julie. They have one daughter, Ashley.

Acknowledgments

Thanks a million, Mom

Special Thanks to: My wife Julie and daughter Ashley. My mother Doris Wamsley, Wally Fetty, my sister Joee Dale and family, Mike, Haley and Katherine Simpson, my late grandfather Henry M. Yester, Richard and Shirley Vanco, Bonnie Watson, Benji, Brandi, Garret and Elizabeth Mcguire, Rick, Melanie and Noah Vanco, Chris Watts, and everyone else who have supported and been there for me.

Additional Thanks to:

Mark Phillips
Carolin Harris
Butch and Bernie at Kittanning Foodland
John Keel
Gary Gibeaut
Natalie "Orbyss" Grewe
Aric Slater
Lisa McIntosh
Barry Conrad
Linda Scarberry
Rosemary Guilley
Sheridan Cleland
Robert Goerman
Ruth and Rush Finley at the Lowe Hotel
Gene Simmons
John and Tim Frick
Donnie Sergent Jr.
Charles Humphreys
Susan Sheppard
Denny Bellamy

Mason County Tourism
Bill Clements and WV Book Company
Mary Skog
Steve Pyles and Dynamic Design crew
WV State Farm Museum staff
Bob Bosworth
Dottie Cambell
Tom Ury
Marcella Bennett
Shirley Hensley
Merle Partridge
Faye Dewitt
Lawrence Gray
Curt Clonch
Darren Hayes
Dolly Grady
Saucer Smear
Mason County Fair Office
Mothmanlives.com list members

Made in the USA
Columbia, SC
21 November 2023